A WICKET OF LIES

A COTSWOLD ANTIQUE MYSTERY

VICTORIA TAIT

KANGA PRESS

A Kanga Press Publication © 2025

Cover Design by Daniela Colleo of StunningBookCovers.com
Editing Allie Douglas

For more information visit VictoriaTait.com

CHAPTER ONE

DOTTY

"Lot 165, a 1948 wooden cricket bat signed by captain Donald Bradman and his Australian 'Invincibles' team who toured England and were unbeaten. Who'll start me off at £150?" asked dark-haired Zach Farmer. His strong but pleasant voice carried an American accent.

Beside him, thirty-one-year-old Dotty Sayers tapped a key on her laptop, glancing up to check that the image on the screen behind them had changed to show the wooden bat.

"£100?" called Zach, but no bids appeared on Dotty's monitor.

"£90?"

Dotty sensed movement in the gathering of auction and sports memorabilia enthusiasts seated in neat rows of white chairs facing the raised stage. As the recently appointed manager of Akemans auction house, she was relieved the auction was taking place at all and delighted that so many had turned up in person to support them.

Even Adrian Cartwright, the deputy headmaster of the school where the auction was being held, was present. He sat nonchalantly at the end of the fourth row, his stocky, bordering on overweight, frame spilling out over the upright chair. His round face appeared relaxed beneath his beard and moustache.

Lazily, he raised his arm, the worn elbow patch of his tweed jacket clearly visible, and held up his auction catalogue, signalling to Zach that he was bidding.

"Thank you," Zach said, and instantly the screen in front of Dotty sprang to life.

£95. £100. £105.

When the unseen internet bidders stopped, Dotty and Zach both looked towards the auction attendees. Adrian Cartwright raised his catalogue again.

The bidding continued steadily.

The large white tent, or marquee to give it its formal name, where this June's auction was taking place was not Akemans' usual venue. But it made a bright and pleasant change, particularly with the floral decorations from Ashcombe Manor School's leavers' dinner and speech day adorning the space.

The scent of lilies and roses mingled with freshly mown grass, drifting in from the nearby cricket pitch. Whenever Dotty had visited this prestigious public school to prepare for the auction, she had seen the same rich-brown-skinned groundsman tending the grass. But then, the Cotswolds' Annual Cricket Festival, held at the school, was only a few weeks away.

"Any more bids?" Zach asked.

Dotty glanced at her screen. The bidding had stopped at £320.

She raised her head, scanning the room. Among the attendees, she spotted several regulars from their usual auctions in the converted flour mill near the Cotswold village of Coln Akeman, along with a scattering of new faces.

Zach began lifting his gavel as a murmur of anticipation spread through the tent. A tall man, wearing a pink open-necked shirt and dark jeans with casual elegance, stepped into the marquee opening.

Looking towards Dotty and Zach, and beyond them to the image on the screen, he raised his arm. His action could have been mistaken for a casual wave, but Zach, who had auctioneered several times since being drafted into the role at the beginning of the year, identified the deliberateness behind it.

"New bidder. £330," Zach stated.

Several people seated towards the front of the marquee turned to see who the newcomer was.

Adrian Cartwright glanced casually behind him, and then his body tensed. As he turned back towards the auctioneer's rostrum, Dotty noticed the set expression on his face as he sat up straighter. He raised his catalogue.

"£340," acknowledged Zach.

Dotty and the rest of the auction audience watched with fascination as the bidding between the two men gained momentum, quickly rising to £2,300. That exceeded their valuation of £1,500 to £2,000. The seller would be happy, and so was Dotty, as their 25% commission on top of the sale price was increasing with each bid.

In his seat, Adrian Cartwright looked uncomfortable as he ran a hand through his already dishevelled sandy-coloured hair.

Zach looked at him and said, "Your bid," in a polite but professional tone.

Adrian was slow to lift his catalogue, and Dotty sensed his reluctance.

"£2,400," said Zach, turning towards the tall man at the back, who still appeared relaxed. The man glanced at the people who had gravitated towards him and smiled appreciatively before staring straight at Zach and calling, "£3,000."

Several people clapped or 'oohed' their appreciation, but Adrian Cartwright wasn't one of them. His face turned a deep plum colour, and he pushed himself up from his chair and waddled out of the marquee without acknowledging the winning bidder.

"Sold," Zach declared, bringing down his gavel and smiling at the new owner of the bat, who was being congratulated by several people.

"I don't have a paddle number," the man called across. "Just put my name down. Gifford Rivers."

Dotty noticed that those who hadn't previously looked to see who'd been bidding were now craning their necks. She bowed her head and wrote Gifford Rivers on the sheet, along with the sale price.

"And now we'll take a ten-minute break before the horse-racing section of the auction," Zach announced before switching off the microphone.

Clara, Akemans' receptionist and trainee antiques specialist, appeared carrying a jug of homemade lemonade. Marion, one of their experts, followed with a tray of glasses and a plate of sandwiches.

Clara was grinning as she gushed, "Wasn't that exciting? And to have Gifford Rivers turn up in person and bid!"

"I saw that sports journalist, Clare Savage, scribbling furiously the moment he raised his hand," Marion added.

Dotty bit thoughtfully into a cucumber and cream cheese sandwich as Zach asked, "Who is our winning bidder? He has the air of a local celebrity."

"Oh, he is," Clara replied enthusiastically. "He runs a local tech company called Gifford Sports Analysis."

"Is that the one sponsoring the Three Counties Ladies' Cricket Cup?" asked Dotty.

She'd been roped into playing cricket for the newly formed village team, The Coln Akeman Larks, even though she struggled to hold the bat the right way up, never mind hit anything. Mostly, she just prayed that the ball, which moved far too fast for her liking, wouldn't strike her instead of the three wooden posts behind her, or wickets, to give them their proper name.

She enjoyed watching cricket matches, especially on warm, lazy, sunny days. And she was happy to provide cakes and sandwiches for the players and their supporters. But to actually play?

She shuddered, thinking of the practice session scheduled for that evening. Could she lie and get out of it, claiming she had too much work to do from the auction? No, that wasn't the right thing to do.

"Yes," Clara said, sounding impressed. "And I hope I get a chance to meet him." Clara was also a member of the ladies' cricket team.

"Gifford Rivers was a schoolboy cricket star and destined for great things," Marion revealed.

"I sense there's a but," said Zach, taking a ham and mustard sandwich.

"Something happened. A scandal." Marion appeared to be trying to recall what it was. "I'm sure there was a woman involved." Then she shook her head, apparently unable to remember any more, and looked at Clara. "And you can meet Gifford now. We need his payment details for that bat."

Clara grinned. "Leave it to me."

CHAPTER TWO

KEYA

"Is that everything?" asked an excited Keya Varma. She loved cricket practice. She loved cricket. She was fully aware there were better players on their recently formed Coln Akeman Larks team, but few of the other ladies were as enthusiastic about the game as she was.

It helped that her boyfriend Sujin Kerr—though she supposed partner was now the better word—was the team's coach.

And it was a wonderful, warm Thursday evening. The perfect end to what had been a busy day at her Waterwheel Cafe.

"There's one more bag with pads and balls. Just there, at the back," said Sujin, who had already hoisted a heavy bag of bats over his shoulder. Another large bag lay at his feet.

Sujin wasn't the tallest, but he was strong, with tawny skin and sharp eyes behind his black-framed, wayfarer-style glasses.

Keya leaned into the rear of Sujin's practical but small 4x4 and hauled out a long canvas bag with Gifford Sports Analysis printed on it.

All the teams taking part in the inaugural Three Counties Ladies' Cricket Cup had been given equipment to encourage them to form teams and help them practise for the competition.

Keya undid her ponytail, letting her straight black hair fall loose for a moment before tying it up again.

"Ready?" Sujin asked, trying to hide his impatience.

"Coming," said Keya with a grin, picking up the long blue bag. She also collected her bright pink one, which Sujin had given her, hoping she wouldn't misplace her kit if it was in such a gaudy colour.

But she liked it, and her grin widened as she followed him to the modern, single-storey brick changing rooms and clubhouse.

"I'll just dump my stuff here," Keya called to Sujin's back as he continued walking.

Two young women pushed open the clubhouse door.

"Hi," they greeted Keya.

Bryonie, the older of the two, said, "Thanks for letting Mum leave work early to pick me up. My bus was cancelled, and I didn't want to miss practice."

"Of course not," Keya replied.

Bryonie attended college in Oxford and worked weekends and holidays at Keya's cafe, where her mother, Alison, was a waitress.

"Let's go to the nets," Bryonie suggested to her younger companion, sixteen-year-old Olivia, whose mother, Gilly, ran Akemans antique centre.

Keya deposited her pink kit bag beside the front door and carried the larger bag around the side of the clubhouse.

Coln Akeman's village cricket pitch was located on the edge of the Cotswold village, on the way to the converted flour mill that housed Akemans Antique Centre and Auction House. That was where Keya ran her Waterwheel Café. As at the café, the River Coln flowed beside the cricket pitch, adding a tranquil and picturesque feel to the setting.

"Hi, sis. Do you need any help?"

Keya looked up as her younger sister, Zivah, walked towards her. She was carrying her batting gloves inside her blue helmet, and a bat was tucked under her arm.

"Thanks, but it's not that heavy. Just a bit unwieldy. Is that your own kit?"

Zivah blushed self-consciously. "Aadi insisted on buying it for me after our last match. He was convinced I'd have scored higher if I'd had my own bat rather than one of the team ones."

"You still scored a half-century," Keya replied. "And without that, we'd have lost." She tilted her head and added, "But I think it's great that your husband is invested in your sporting achievements and is prepared to buy you new kit as well as look after Kaami. How is my baby nephew, by the way?"

"He's hardly a baby anymore. He's already pulling himself up onto his feet, and before long, he'll be charging around. I'm not sure how I'll keep up with him."

Keya raised her eyebrows as she regarded her sister's slim, fit figure. But then, Zivah was on her feet all day in her role as front-of-house at the Waterwheel Cafe.

"I'd better take this kit to Sujin," Keya said as she spotted him looking in their direction.

She stepped out onto the circular grass cricket field, roughly a hundred metres in diameter, its boundary marked by slightly faded white paint.

She'd thought the whole area was called a pitch, but Sujin had told her it wasn't quite so simple. The pitch was the central rectangular area where the two batsmen—or batswomen—stood. It was marked by shorter grass and three knee-high posts, at each end, called wickets.

As she reached Sujin, who'd already put the wicket's three wooden stumps in place, he said, "Can you see if someone put the bails in your bag?"

Keya unzipped the blue bag, knelt down, and rooted around until she found four short pieces of wood, which she handed to Sujin.

"Thanks," he said, placing two bails across the top of the three stumps closest to them. Then he walked down the pitch to the batting crease at the other end and repeated the action, setting the remaining two bails in place.

Keya looked wistfully at the wicket closest to her. She rarely bowled straight enough to hit it, and even when she did, most players easily knocked her balls away.

Then she smiled affectionately. All except her best friend, Dotty, who cowered in front of the stumps, holding her bat out in front of her like a protective shield.

Poor Dotty. She really did hate playing, but every time Sujin asked if she wanted to step down, she shook her head resolutely and carried on. But Keya knew she was lying when she said at the end of each practice how much she'd enjoyed the session. She was only playing because there was nobody else, and she didn't want to let the team down.

As Keya thought of Dotty, she heard her voice and looked up.

Dotty was walking slowly across the pitch, dressed in a pair of navy cotton shorts with a blue and white striped top. She was accompanied by Clara and Marion from the auction house, and Aunt Beanie.

Aunt Beanie was a colourful and rather eccentric figure, renowned for her strong opinions and for holding back her long silver-white hair with a series of brightly coloured scarves. Today's scarf was red, matching her T-shirt, which read: "Sassy, Classy, And A Little Bit Bad-Assy."

"Nice T-shirt," called Olivia from the direction of the cricket nets, grinning.

Of all the people who called her Aunt Beanie, Olivia was the only one actually related to her. Keya supposed that made Olivia the older woman's great-niece, if there was such a term.

"And I got to meet Gifford Rivers," Clara said, blushing slightly as the group of women approached the centre of the field.

"So it was a successful auction?" asked Aunt Beanie.

"We couldn't have asked for more," Dotty replied. "Not with our premises being out of bounds due to construction work. And Zach's suggestion of theming it as a special sports memorabilia sale was an excellent idea. It attracted a different group of buyers. Limiting the auction to smaller pieces of furniture also meant fewer items to transport."

"And we managed to create an attractive display in just two days between the school's Leavers' Dinner and their Speech Day," added Marion. "It looked very elegant, even if I say so myself."

"I only hope we can get back into Akeman's auction room for July's sale, as we now have a backlog of large items in the storage rooms," Dotty said with a sigh.

"I still think you could conduct an auction in there now that partitions have been put in to divide the space, and it's been painted and fitted out with new lighting," Aunt Beanie responded.

"We'll see," Dotty replied as they reached Keya and Sujin.

"Busy day?" Keya asked.

"Yes, but an exciting one," Clara answered with a smile.

"We should get started," Sujin said, approaching the group.

"Then I better get myself sorted," Keya replied, striding back across the cricket field.

She collected her bag and headed towards the changing rooms. They were using the men's, as the ladies' could only fit four people in at a squeeze. Stripping off her outer layers, she changed into a pair of fitted three-quarter length black Lycra leggings with a pink stripe and a matching T-shirt before making her way back outside.

As she left the clubhouse, she bumped into two more cricket team members, friends Melanie Carter and Tani Hargreaves. Both were in their mid-thirties and lived and worked in Coln Akeman.

Mel, who served behind the bar at The Axeman pub, was wearing a tight-fitting T-shirt with 'Why Be Modest When You Look This Good?' stretched across her ample chest, and a pair of very brief shorts that clung to her legs.

Tani, rake thin and trying to mask her exhaustion beneath thick make-up, juggled being a single mum to two young children while working part-time at the Post Office.

"I like your hair," Keya said as she joined the two women, walking across the cricket field with them.

"Thanks," said Tani, flicking her long ponytail of dyed icy-blonde hair.

"I did it," Mel said, with a touch of sulkiness. "What do you think of the plaits?"

"Excellent. Very neat," Keya replied, pasting on what she hoped was a genuine smile. She struggled to warm to Mel, but she had to admit, the plaits were well done. Four tight braids ran across Tani's head, feeding into the base of her ponytail, where the contrast between her natural dark roots and the stark blonde dye was most noticeable.

"That's everyone. Brilliant," Sujin said, glancing over at the final arrival.

Georgina Carey, who was Olivia's aunt and Aunt Beanie's niece, arrived slightly out of breath and apologised, "Sorry I'm late."

"No problem," Sujin replied. "But before we start practising, I want us to think about Sunday's match. You've done amazingly well to reach the semi-finals, and it will be a tough game against the Hereford

Hinds. Win that, and you'll secure your place at the Cotswolds' Summer Cricket Festival."

"And meet Gifford Rivers," said Tani in a dreamy voice.

Clara leaned in and murmured, "I met him today, at our auction."

"I don't know what you see in him," muttered Mel, eyeing Zach, who was striding purposefully across the cricket field towards them.

Keya caught the look and was pleased to see Dotty had noticed it too. Her friend's mouth tightened, and a small crease appeared between her brows before she quickly looked down. Dotty really did need to sort herself out when it came to Zach. Denying her feelings was only going to push him away.

CHAPTER THREE

DOTTY

Dotty took a deep breath and, standing sideways in front of the wicket, settled her feet hip-width apart, bending her knees slightly. Sujin had taught her this was the best way to maintain her balance and stability.

He'd also told her to hold the bat lightly, but she gripped it tightly with her padded gloves, arms locked, bat angled forward. With any luck, the ball would strike it before hitting her.

She adjusted her uncomfortable helmet.

At least she was facing Keya. So far, only one of the three balls her friend had bowled had come directly at her.

The rest of the team crowded round the pitch instead of spreading out across the field, partly because any ball she hit wouldn't go far and partly, she suspected, to intercept Keya's unpredictable bowling.

"Just relax," Zach murmured, close behind her. Although he knew nothing about cricket, he was helping Sujin and managing the team's other needs, which he insisted was necessary since Akemans and Keya's Waterwheel Cafe were sponsoring them.

Keya sprinted towards the far wicket, and Dotty felt her whole body tense. Releasing the ball, Keya came to a stop and then stood with her hands on her hips, as she pinched her lips together in frustration.

"Wide," Zach called as Dotty breathed out in relief.

Only two more balls left in this over, but then she might have to face Aunt Beanie or Zivah. Zivah bowled straight and fast, whereas Aunt Beanie's balls were wildly unpredictable, spinning in all directions and catching batters out. It was fun to watch, but not to be on the receiving end.

As Keya walked back to the start of her run-up, Dotty stood taller and stretched her back. She saw that several local people were strolling round the ground or standing to watch the practice. The local villagers had been surprisingly supportive of home matches, but perhaps that was because the team put on an excellent tea and The Axeman pub offered every spectator a free drink.

Keya turned to face the crease, and Dotty prepared herself again.

The ball came at her slower than Keya's other balls, but straighter.

"Step into it and move the bat through," Zach instructed.

Dotty kept her eyes firmly on the hard, spinning red ball and instinctively, more for protection than anything else, she stepped forward and struck the ball away. It sailed over the heads of the fielders and rolled across the field.

"Well done! Fantastic shot," Zach praised.

Dotty felt her cheeks burning. There hadn't been any skill to her stroke. Just self-preservation.

Mel, the closest fielder, walked unenthusiastically towards the ball just as a small black and tan terrier ran onto the field, yapping with delight. It sprinted straight to the ball, but after realising it was too large to collect in its mouth, it used its nose to nudge it instead.

"Hello, Willow," Mel said, squatting down to pet the small dog. "Do you want to play too?"

"I'm so sorry," a short woman wearing a baseball cap called as she strode across the grass, lead in hand. "I didn't think he'd chase the ball."

"I wasn't expecting him to have a ball to chase, Pip," Mel replied. "That's the first time Dotty has actually hit it."

Dotty's cheeks burned hotter, and she scuffed the bare patch of earth in front of the wicket with the toe of her trainer.

"Don't take any notice," Zach reassured her.

She turned and looked up into his smiling face.

"That was a great shot. Same again this ball?" he encouraged.

Dotty nodded uncertainly as Mel threw the ball back to Keya. She had an incredibly strong throw.

Pip, the woman in the baseball cap, scooped up the terrier and walked back across the field to where a tall, slightly chubby man with glasses was waiting for her.

Dotty prepared herself for the last ball of Keya's over.

Perhaps inspired by her previous ball, Keya ran in more quickly this time, but her delivery was still straight and long.

Dotty hesitated, unsure whether to step forward to meet the ball or back away from it.

Panicking, she stepped back just as the fast-paced ball bounced on the ground in front of her and rose sharply.

She tried to duck, but the ball kept rising and… whack.

The evening sky was such a soft blue, she thought as her eyes focused on it. But why was she looking up at the sky?

Ow. And why did her head hurt? Had she fallen over?

Then she heard the clamour of voices and felt the lumpy earth beneath her back.

"Dotty!" Keya cried. "Oh, thank goodness. You're awake."

"I'm fine," Dotty mumbled, trying to sit up.

"No, you're not," said Zach's tender but firm voice as he squatted down to support her. "At the very least you'll have a pounding headache, but I wouldn't be surprised if you have concussion. It was a good ball though, Keya. One of your best."

"But…" Keya's eyes were wide with worry.

"No, it was my fault," Dotty said, sitting upright and bracing her hands against the short grass behind her. "I panicked and stepped back rather than forward to meet the ball."

"Do you want someone to call Dr Peter?" asked Aunt Beanie, her voice as commanding and practical as ever.

"Dad said he was coming to watch the end of practice and walk home with me," said Olivia, whose father was the local doctor.

"Then why don't I help Dotty back to the clubhouse and wait for him?" Zach offered.

"But the team… they'll be one short," Dotty protested.

"Not a problem for tonight," Sujin replied. "Right, Zivah, you bat, and Bryonie can take a turn at bowling."

As Sujin reorganised his practice, Zach helped Dotty carefully to her feet and they slowly made their way across the cricket field.

Dotty felt dizzy at first and had to lean on Zach's strong, athletic frame.

"You were very brave," Zach said in a gentle tone. "Everyone knows you hate playing and that you only carried on so you wouldn't let the side down. Literally."

"Do you think I'll be able to play on Sunday, for the semi-final match?" Dotty asked, her brow furrowing. She really didn't want to disappoint the team.

"I'm not sure, but I don't think you should. The Hereford Hinds have several fast bowlers and…"

"I might panic again," muttered Dotty. She was annoyed with herself. Everyone else was able to play and actually enjoyed the matches. Why was she so hopeless?

"Stop beating yourself up," Zach said as they reached the clubhouse and sat down on the front row of plastic seats in front of it.

The couple with the terrier who'd rushed onto the pitch earlier were sitting further along the row.

"So cricket isn't your game. That's nothing to be ashamed of. There's no point pretending to yourself or the rest of us that you want to play. Besides, if you're injured, who'll bake all the wonderful cakes for cricket tea?"

"Mick from Keya's cafe does most of that now, but…"

A ripple of applause spread through the spectators as the ball soared over the field. Dotty noticed that the fielders were more spread out than when she'd been batting, but even so, the ball Zivah hit sailed over their heads.

The terrier yapped, wriggled, and then broke free from the bespectacled man's grasp. It dashed along the side of the pitch and snuffled about in a flowerbed until it found the ball.

"Well done, Willow," said Pip, jogging after the excited dog.

She picked the ball out from beside a flowering lavender bush, took a step forward, and threw it long and straight.

Olivia, the wicketkeeper, who wore extra pads and gloves, tried to stop the ball, but it bounced off her leg pad. She scrambled after it.

"What a throw," Zach observed. "She should be in the team."

Dotty wondered if Sujin had thought the same as he strode across the field towards them.

"Excuse me," he said as the couple with the terrier made to leave. "That was an amazing throw. We're a player down now for our ladies' side, and we have an important match on Sunday. Do you think you could step in? We've tried everyone else in the village, and besides, none of them has an arm like yours. Why didn't you come to the trials?"

"We only moved to the village recently," replied the man. "I'm Ned, by the way. Ned Pritchard, and this is my fiancée, Philippa."

"Pip," corrected the woman. "I… I'm really not sure…"

"Oh, come on, Pip. You've said you'd like to get more involved in village activities, and you enjoy watching cricket on the telly. Why not give it a go?"

"Yes, help us out!" called a male voice from behind Dotty.

"We'll need someone who can throw like you when we face the Hereford Hinds," commented another.

"Go on," Ned encouraged.

"At least come and meet the team and throw the ball around," Sujin suggested.

"But what about supper?" protested Pip.

"I can see to that, or we can grab a bite at the pub. Besides, it's a lovely evening, and there's no rush."

Pip looked around at the expectant, encouraging faces of the onlookers.

Sighing deeply, her shoulders slumped as she reluctantly followed Sujin onto the cricket field.

CHAPTER FOUR

DOTTY

The next morning, Dotty sat in the large, sunlit kitchen at Meadowbank Farm, on the edge of the Cotswold town of Fairford, nursing a cup of English Breakfast tea. She needed to clear her head, which still felt rather fuzzy.

Although she loved the warmth of the sun, she'd had to sit at the large, rectangular pine kitchen table with her back to the conservatory section of the room, as the light from the full-height windows made her squint, sending a sharp pain across her temple.

Her furry grey cat, Earl Grey, was purring gently on her lap. Stroking him, she murmured, "You haven't been getting much attention recently, have you? But I've been so busy running the auction house and dealing with the repairs and the building work. At least we don't have to worry about cricket practice anymore. Although, I still need to support the team."

She looked up quickly as the kitchen door opened and winced with pain. She'd woken up with a dull, throbbing headache, but when she moved, a sharp pain tightened around her skull.

"You've done more than enough," said Aunt Beanie, stepping into the kitchen with a small bunch of delicate sweet peas. Their soft, ruffled petals ranged from pale pinks and purples to soft whites, and their heady, honey-like fragrance immediately filled the room.

As she placed them in a small cut-glass vase, she asked, "Did I hear Zach padding about?"

"Yes," Dotty replied. "He insisted on staying in the spare room in case I had any funny turns in the night." She tried to smile, but even that was too sore. "He's just taking a shower, and then he'll grab a quick breakfast before heading to a meeting with the architect at Akemans. I suppose I should get up and make him something."

"You stay where you are. You're far too unsteady on your feet to be doing anything this morning. What you need to do is rest."

"But we have all the invoices and the sale items from the auction to sort out. And anything not taken from Ashcombe Manor School yesterday has to be brought back to Akemans for collection or delivery."

She stopped as a wave of nausea swept over her, making her stomach churn and her head spin.

"Leave that to Marion and Clara. They're quite capable of sorting everything out. What they don't need is to be looking after you if you collapse or continue feeling dizzy and nauseous."

Dotty's eyes widened in surprise and she felt Earl Grey tense on her lap.

"Don't you think I've had concussion before?" Aunt Beanie said as she placed the small vase of sweet peas in the centre of the pine table. "I remember…"

But her reminiscences were cut short as Zach entered the kitchen from the direction of Dotty's adjoining cottage, which had an interconnecting door to the main farmhouse.

His hair was damp, and he was clean-shaven. The sharp scent of his aftershave mingled with the delicate fragrance of the sweet peas.

"Are you in a rush?" Aunt Beanie asked, "or shall I put some sausages in the oven? I bought some lovely pork and leek ones at the farmers' market on Tuesday."

"I've pushed back my morning meeting, so yes, that would be lovely," Zach replied.

Dotty continued stroking the appreciative Earl Grey as Aunt Beanie sorted out a tray of sausages and Zach made himself a cup of coffee.

When Aunt Beanie had placed the tray in the top oven of her blue Aga range cooker, she said, "I'm just popping out to feed the sheep.

The sausages should be fine, but can you keep an eye on them, Zach?"

She pointedly said his name while staring at Dotty.

Zach sat down at the kitchen table with his cup of coffee and asked, "How are you?"

"Groggy. And I feel both stupid and useless for letting a cricket ball hit me. And from Keya?"

"It was a superb ball and pitched long," Zach replied seriously.

Despite the pain, Dotty smiled. He'd thrown himself completely into cricket since they'd been asked to put together a local ladies' team for the summer tournament. She'd been surprised when he'd suggested that they and Keya also sponsor the team, but Zach had reasoned that many of the players were involved with both businesses.

After the allegations of impropriety earlier in the year, they needed to boost Akemans' reputation. And she had to admit, supporting a women's sport gave them a softer, more community-focused image.

"I presume you're not going into work today?" Zach enquired.

"I want to, but Aunt Beanie was hinting that I'd be more of a liability than a help."

Zach smiled sympathetically, but then his expression tightened.

"What is it?" Dotty asked. "Is there an issue with the building work?"

"No, it's nothing to do with Akemans or work, and I didn't really want to bring it up while you're feeling under the weather, but I have a meeting with the rental agency this afternoon."

"Oh," Dotty said in surprise.

"You remember I told you I'd taken a six-month lease on the house in Burford? Well, that runs out next month, and I have to give them a month's notice, either to leave or extend."

"But it's a lovely house, especially now the garden has come to life. And the apple trees will be full of fruit this autumn."

"I know, but there are other houses… and other places."

"But I thought… now that you're running Akemans… and the building work. And what about your plans for the business?"

"All my plans centre on you. I've told you that." Zach's voice was steady and serious. "As I said, this isn't the ideal time to talk about it, but I've been trying for weeks, and you've always been busy. It's crunch time. I have to make a decision."

Dotty's head spun, and she didn't think it was purely from the cricket ball. A knot tightened in her stomach.

"I… oh, I don't feel great." Dotty stood, gripping the table for support, and spilling Earl Grey onto the floor.

Zach jumped up to help her. "I knew I shouldn't have said anything, but time has run out."

Dotty felt herself reel. She blurted out, "I think I'm going to be sick."

CHAPTER FIVE

KEYA

"It's a lovely sunny day!" Keya exclaimed brightly on Sunday morning as she pulled back the heavy cotton curtains, their bold blue and sand-coloured geometric patterns set against a rich red background.

"What time is it?" moaned Sujin, covering his eyes with his hand.

"Seven," Keya replied. "I need to get to the cafe early to set up for the day before I leave for the cricket match. Mick's also coming in first thing to finish making the sandwiches and bakes for today's match tea."

"Did you have to wake me so early?"

"Oh, stop complaining," Keya teased as she bounced back onto the bed and lay down on the duvet next to Sujin.

"Nobody can stay asleep on a day like today! The sun, the excitement of the match… just think, if we win, we'll be playing at the Cotswold Summer Cricket Festival, in front of a proper crowd." Her eyes shone brightly.

"I know that, and it would be an amazing achievement, but the Hereford Hinds are a top team. This is their third season playing, and they have far more resources than we do. We're literally down to our last man… or should I say woman."

"Don't be so negative. We have a great team, and a great coach." She leaned down and squeezed him tightly.

Letting go, she announced, "And now I need to sort myself out." She padded barefoot across the whitewashed wooden floor, enjoying the soft texture of the woven turquoise rug beneath her feet. As she reached their recently converted en-suite shower room, she turned back and asked,

"And can you take my kit with you? I'll go straight from the cafe."

Keya's Waterwheel Cafe was at the rear of the ground floor of a three-storey converted flour mill, less than a mile from Coln Akeman.

Dotty managed the auction house, which usually conducted its business out of the adjoining single-storey building, but that was currently covered in a tangled web of metal scaffolding poles.

Zach had recently been appointed Managing Director of Akemans antique and auction house, and his first job was to ensure the structural integrity of the old mill buildings.

Keya had also heard Dotty mention that he was investing some of his own money into the business so they could modernise the auction house, improve the antique centre, and convert some of the currently unused space.

Keya walked through the closed antique centre to reach her cafe. The stalls were set up as usual, their displays undisturbed, waiting for the day's customers. With no people around and only a few dim lights on, the space felt strangely still. It always made her skin prickle. What history did this building hold? What stories of joy, tragedy, and hard work could the walls tell?

She shivered as she opened the interconnecting door and stepped into her cafe. Although the hanging metal dome pendant lights were off, light flooded through the full-height windows overlooking the working waterwheel and the River Coln. The French doors, which led out onto the riverbank and outdoor seating area, were open, allowing the warm summer air to drift in and refresh the cafe space.

From the direction of the kitchen, she could hear music, and was that singing? She weaved her way between the tables and chairs, drawn towards the sound.

"Trailers for sale or rent, rooms to let, fifty cents..." Mick Gospel sang softly as he worked.

He was a large man, his presence imposing despite his quiet nature. Years of wrongful imprisonment had left him self-effacing and hardworking, and he preferred to keep himself to himself. He looked menacing to some, especially with his recently shaved head, which was perhaps an attempt to disguise his greying hair, and the tattoos covering his arms.

He had dreams of travelling the world but, so far, he'd only visited Morocco the previous January. As Keya watched him remove a large aluminium baking tray from the oven, she wondered if he had plans for another trip. He wasn't secretive about what he did or what he hoped to do, but he rarely spoke about it.

"That smells wonderful," enthused Keya. "What is it?"

"I found a recipe in a magazine and thought I'd use up the last of the raspberries to make a tray of raspberry custard slices."

"Great idea! But can I smell almonds?"

"Yes, and I'm going to sprinkle some flaked pieces on top."

"That'll help identify it for people with nut allergies, but I'll also make sure I take one of our 'contains nuts' cards with us to make it clear. What else needs doing?" Keya asked.

"I've weighed out the ingredients for the flapjack," Mick said, turning away from the tray and moving to a counter where a bowl of porridge oats sat on the scales. Beside it, a large pan contained a knob of butter, and a mix of golden syrup and light brown sugar.

"I'll melt this down and then fold in the oats," Mick explained as he placed the pan on the hob.

Keya knew he was reluctant to give her or anyone else instructions, so she searched for the picnic preparation list and found it sitting on the open hatch between the kitchen and the cafe.

There were a range of sandwiches to prepare.

"I'll start on the ham, mustard, and lettuce sandwiches," Keya suggested.

An hour or so later, Keya had made all the ham and mustard sandwiches, as well as the cream cheese and chive ones. As she started peeling the eggs she had already hard-boiled, she heard the cafe door open.

Ducking down so she could see through the hatch, she spotted Dotty taking the long route around the tables, and she was carrying two heavy-looking wicker baskets.

"Hiya," Keya called, stepping out of the kitchen.

"Morning. Do you mind if I finish preparing my picnic items for the cricket tea here? Aunt Beanie has lost her lucky pair of socks and is in a right tizz. Norman is helping her look for them, but I know he needs to be here soon."

"You're right," Keya said, suddenly remembering she needed to open the cafe. "Mick, when you've finished packing the tray bakes, can you peel the eggs? Oh, but before you do that, you'd better check we have enough bacon out for sandwiches this morning."

"I've already done that. There's a new packet in the fridge," Mick confirmed.

"Thanks," Keya replied as she washed her hands.

"Why don't you two sort out the cafe while I carry on with the picnic?" Dotty suggested. "And can I borrow your grill for the chicken satay skewers? I couldn't cook them in the Aga at Meadowbank Farm."

"Yes, of course," said Keya distractedly. As she left the kitchen, she heard Mick ask, "What are Aunt Beanie's lucky socks?"

Keya knew they were a light-green and red diamond-patterned pair, which were completely inappropriate and not in keeping with the plain white socks they were supposed to wear for cricket. But Sujin had long since given up asking Aunt Beanie to wear the right kit.

She hoped the socks had been found because she really did need Norman at the cafe soon to start making hot drinks. He had initially moved into Meadowbank Farm to help Aunt Beanie care for her late husband. After spending most of his life working outdoors for a local aristocrat, he had taken the position as porter at the auction house, and later trained as a barista at the cafe.

He was also a steadying hand, and his watchful gaze kept an eye on customers. Not that her usuals caused much trouble, but when coach parties visited the antique centre…

"Sorry I'm late," Norman apologised, cutting through her train of thought.

His permanently tanned face, with its broken veins, creased into a warm smile. She noticed that he'd recently trimmed his hair, moustache, and beard. Although at least twenty years older than Mick, Keya wondered if he was also trying to hide the fact that his sandy hair had a silver tinge to it.

"No problem. Did you find Aunt Beanie's socks?"

Norman rolled his eyes. "They were at the bottom of the laundry basket, but she's insisting on wearing them. If the Coln Akeman Larks are losing, we can knock the other team out with the smell of Bernadette's feet!"

Norman started organising himself for the morning.

Back in the kitchen, Keya found Dotty mashing the pile of hard-boiled eggs with a mixture of mayonnaise, salad cream, and a hint of mustard.

"How are you feeling?" she asked. She hadn't had a proper conversation with Dotty since accidentally hitting her on the head with a cricket ball. "I really am sorry about my bowling."

"Your bowling was fine. In fact, it was excellent. It's just that..." Dotty's voice trailed off.

"You're not a cricket player?" suggested Keya.

"Exactly, and it's such a relief I don't have to pretend anymore. Pip can throw better than me, and she's bound to be better with a bat, even if she doesn't bowl." Dotty sighed. "It's a huge relief not to be playing."

"Then why the glum expression?" asked Keya, feeling her own bright mood fading.

Dotty looked up at her, lips pressed together.

"What?" And then Keya nodded. "It's Zach, isn't it? He's been a bit distant this past week. I thought it was just an issue with the building works. But have you two had an argument?"

"No," Dotty replied defensively, and then she winced. Was her head still sore from Thursday's accident?

"Then what? Something isn't adding up." Keya didn't believe in beating around the bush or making small talk when it came to those closest to her. Problems had to be tackled head-on.

"Do you remember I said he'd given me six months to make up my mind about whether we had a future together?"

"Yes, and that was at the end of January, so… oh, you only have a month left."

"Not even that," replied Dotty despondently. "He's to give a month's notice on his house in Burford to leave or stay, so he wants an answer now."

"So why don't you give him one?"

"Because I don't know what to do!"

CHAPTER SIX

DOTTY

Dotty hadn't meant to blurt out her anxiety over Zach and the huge decision he wanted her to make, but she felt relieved when she did.

She was sure Keya was about to suggest they talk about it when voices interrupted them, and Monica and Alison arrived. Monica worked with Mick in the kitchen, and Alison who was Bryonie's mum, was a waitress.

Then Norman called, "It's time to open."

Keya looked at Dotty with a pained expression and apologised. "Sorry, can we discuss this later?"

"Of course," Dotty replied. She certainly didn't want to talk about her love life, or lack of it, in front of so many people.

She finished mixing the egg mayonnaise and began spreading it on sliced white bread to make sandwiches.

"How are you, dear?" asked Marion as she and Dotty climbed out of their cars in the car park behind the clubhouse at the Coln Akeman cricket field.

"Better, thank you. Although I still have a dull headache, and if I move too quickly, I get a sharp pain," Dotty replied.

"If it persists, don't worry about Monday. Clara and I will only be sorting out the few remaining items and payments from the auction."

"Thank you, but we need to arrange what to do about the next one, and for that, I need to speak to Zach..." The words caught in her throat, and she stopped, swallowing hard.

Marion drew closer, carrying a smart leather overnight bag that contained her sports kit. "Are you sure you're all right?" she asked.

Dotty nodded, worried that if she spoke, she'd dissolve into tears. Gathering herself, she lied, "It's just my head."

But of course, she knew it wasn't. It was her heart.

She turned away from Marion to lift her two baskets of picnic items out of the car, and when she turned back, Marion had gone to join Clara, who'd also recently arrived.

Relieved, Dotty carried her baskets not into the clubhouse but around the side of the field to the old cricket pavilion. She loved this small, single-storey building, which reminded her of photos of vintage village cricket matches.

It was a wooden structure with steps leading up to a railed balcony that ran along the front of the pavilion. How many cricket players had sat there, watching their teammates bat, either to victory or defeat?

The building was painted white with green edging and a sloping green tin roof.

Inside, Mel was helping Barry, the landlord of The Axeman pub, set up the bar.

"Morning," Barry greeted her.

Dotty glanced at her watch. The first ball was due to be bowled at half past eleven.

He turned to Mel and said, "That's all right, luv. I can finish off. You'd better get ready for the match."

"Thanks, I do need to make myself look presentable. Is Zach manning the scoreboard?" Mel asked in an innocent voice.

"I presume so," Dotty replied, forcing herself to sound cheerful as she took in the tight fit of Mel's black T-shirt and the shortness of her miniskirt.

Mel flashed a grin at Barry before teetering towards the entrance in high-heeled white shoes.

Barry didn't notice, focused instead on lifting a black crate of beer onto a stack of similar crates.

"I hear you're injured and not playing today. That's a shame," said Barry sympathetically as he organised the crates.

"I don't think it is. Everyone will be far happier having Pip play in my place, including me." Dotty smiled as Barry turned towards her, and then she started setting out the food.

When she returned to her car to fetch the rest of it, she met Keya, and together they walked back to the cricket pavilion carrying sandwiches, cakes and bakes.

As they rounded the corner, Dotty suddenly stopped.

"Watch it!" Keya exclaimed.

But Dotty ignored her, her eyes fixed on Mel, who was leaning against the wall, talking to Zach. She lifted a hand and smoothed down the front of his shirt.

Keya, who had skirted around Dotty as she stood rigid, marched forward, calling, "Come on. We need to finish setting up so I can get a few practice bowls in."

Ahead of them, Zach stepped back, his face colouring.

"Hi," he said to Keya and Dotty, although Dotty was sure his brightness was feigned.

Mel just grinned in a way that reminded Dotty of an expression Aunt Beanie used. She looked like a cat that got the cream.

Dotty was still trying to process whether she'd just witnessed an innocent exchange or something more when Keya said, "Don't read anything into that. It's just Mel flirting. She's not Zach's type."

"But how do you know?" Dotty asked uncertainly.

Keya gave her a knowing look and said, "I'm happy to talk about it, just not now. Later, when I'm waiting to bat."

Coln Akeman Larks lost the toss and the Hereford Hinds opted to field first, meaning the home team were batting. True to her word, Keya left her teammates and, carrying a wooden bat, a blue helmet, and her white gloves and batting pads, she joined Dotty on the balcony of the cricket pavilion.

It was still early, and the atmosphere remained quiet. Spectators were gathered in small groups at the edge of the field, chatting. They hadn't yet drifted towards the pavilion for refreshments.

"Right," Keya said, flopping down onto the moulded plastic chair beside Dotty. "Let's get you sorted. Why are you struggling to make a decision about Zach?"

Dotty hesitated, glancing down at her hands. "I don't know… I mean, I do, but I don't."

Keya raised an eyebrow. "That makes no sense. Try again. You like Zach, and more than just as a friend. I've seen the way you look at him, and you're relaxed together, and happy. So what's stopping you from taking the next step?"

Glancing towards the pitch, she called, "Good block!" as Zivah knocked a defensive shot across the mown grass.

Turning back to Dotty, she added, "I know I'm more impulsive. Sujin and I moving in together just felt right at the time with the boiler breaking down in my rented property, and then being given the house in Tetbury. And I get that you need time to think things through. But it's been over a year, and nearly six months since Zach moved to the Cotswolds. So what exactly is holding you back?"

Suddenly, Keya jumped up and cried, "Great shot!" as Zivah sent the ball soaring over the boundary. An opposition player stopped running after it, waiting instead for a spectator to toss the ball back.

Dotty sighed. "It's just… things with Zach. He's wonderful. Supportive. Strong. I like being around him. But…"

"But?" Keya prompted, her tone gentle but firm as she sat back down.

Dotty stared towards the field, searching for the right words. "I spent years with Al, letting him make all the decisions. Telling me what I should do, how I should spend my time, who I should be. Even what I should wear. And it was such an effort for me to step out of his controlling shadow and learn to do things on my own. To make my own choices."

Keya nodded and then turned to watch her sister who was now facing a fast-paced bowler.

Dotty ploughed on. Now that she'd started, she needed to finish the conversation and, if possible, make a decision.

Even though Keya was distracted by the play, Dotty continued, "I know I need help sometimes, and I can't do everything alone. I don't want to. But at the same time, I don't want to slip back into being that person who just follows along, and who lets someone else take control."

She exhaled. "I guess I'm scared of losing myself again."

"Oh," Keya groaned as a ball skimmed over Zivah's wicket, just high enough that it didn't knock off the bails. Zivah glanced back at it, then turned to face the bowler again, tapping the end of her bat purposefully against the browning grass.

Then, turning her attention back to Dotty, Keya gave her a slow, knowing smile. "So, what you're saying is... you have feelings for Zach, but you don't want him to run your life?"

Dotty breathed out in relief and smiled. "Yes. That's exactly what I mean."

Keya leaned in and whispered, "So just tell him that."

Dotty blinked. "Is it really that simple?"

"Dotty," Keya said, shaking her head with amusement, "if he's really the guy you think he is, he'll get it. And if he doesn't, well... then maybe he's not the right one after all."

Dotty felt some of the weight lift from her chest, and even the ache in her head eased slightly. Maybe it really was as straightforward as that.

Keya jumped to her feet again, cheering as Zivah sent another ball soaring over the boundary.

CHAPTER SEVEN

DOTTY

Dotty sat contentedly beside Keya for a while, watching Zivah and other members of the Coln Akeman Larks bat.

"Thank you," she said to her best friend. "I really appreciate the chat."

"If you really want my advice," Keya said, raising an eyebrow as she glanced at Dotty, "I'd stop worrying about work and the auction house and start focusing a little more on your personal life. If you don't want to lose Zach, and I'm sure you don't, then you not only need to speak to him but show him you mean it. He needs to know you're serious about building a future together. Commitment can be scary, but you're allowed to change your mind if, for some wild reason, you decide Zach's not the man for you. And just watch out. You're not the only one with designs on him."

As Keya spoke, Mel, who had just struck a clean shot along the grass, giving her and Zivah two more runs, looked over at the scoreboard where Zach was updating the score by hand and smiled broadly.

"She has no hesitation showing Zach exactly how she feels about him," Keya said pointedly.

Dotty continued watching as Mel was caught out attempting an ambitious shot, and Tani was next in to bat. Unfortunately, the ball swept past her and smashed the wooden wicket after only two balls. Head bowed, she left the field and was replaced by Clara.

"I'd better go," said Keya. "There's Clara, then Olivia, and then me."

Two well-dressed couples in their sixties allowed Keya to run down the pavilion steps before they climbed up the steps and asked Dotty, "Is the food ready?"

Dotty helped serve them and several more spectators before taking a break again. Instead of sitting down, she leaned against the white painted wooden balustrade which ran along the front of the pavilion.

Keya was right. Not just about being more dynamic and purposeful with Zach and their relationship, but also about worrying less about Akemans. It would sort itself out. After all, Zach was managing the building work, and within the business she had the support of Marion and Clara in the office, Gilly Wimsey at the antique centre, and Keya. And of course, there was also Aunt Beanie, who might be eccentric but she always had an opinion and some different and often excellent ideas.

Clapping around the field jolted her back to the present. In the centre of the field, Zivah raised her wooden bat acknowledging the applause.

Dotty glanced at the scoreboard as Zack slotted 50 into place beside batter one. Zivah had reached her half-century.

Zach looked across the field at Dotty and smiled, giving her the thumbs up sign.

Her inclination was to do nothing but following her conversation with Keya she knew she needed to be more proactive. She raised her right arm and waved in response.

Clara defended solidly, hitting a steady succession of singles, which meant she ran to the far end while Zivah rotated back to face the bowler. Now in her rhythm, Zivah played strongly and confidently. But she wasn't extravagant and didn't take unnecessary chances.

Clara was unlucky to be out when she attempted another quick single. A fielder threw the ball accurately from a distance, striking the wicket before she could reach it.

Next in was Keya. She swung wildly, quickly racking up three fours, where the ball reached the boundary after bouncing or hitting the ground, and one six, which was a wild but powerful hit straight over the boundary rope. Trying to repeat the shot, she was caught out on the next ball.

Dotty realised the team had to be careful. They had five more overs of six balls each, and if they wanted to set a high target for the opposition, Zivah needed to stay in. But she couldn't do it alone. She needed a batting partner. Someone who would play sensibly and conservatively.

That was not Aunt Beanie, who usually batted next. Yet the small, neat figure striding across the field from the clubhouse wasn't Aunt Beanie. Dotty had no idea who was under the blue cricket helmet with its metal face guard. Olivia and Clara had already batted.

The two batters had a brief discussion before the newcomer walked away from Dotty, examined the wicket, then turned and held her bat steady as the bowler ran in.

"I see Sujin's put Pip in to bat. I hope she can cope against this fast-paced bowler," Barry remarked, leaning against the doorframe of the pavilion.

"Good defending," he added as Pip stepped forward, pushing the ball along the ground with her bat. It was a defensive shot, but because of the bowler's pace, the ball ran quickly across the hard ground.

"Run!" Zivah shouted, and the two batters sprinted across the pitch, switching ends.

"If they both keep playing like that, we have a chance of reaching a hundred and fifty runs or more, which I think is the target we need to set for the Hereford Hinds."

Dotty continued watching the match, although she was occasionally interrupted by spectators looking for food.

"Final over," Barry said from the open doorway. "We have a hundred and thirty-five runs, which is solid. I don't think Zivah's going to reach a century which is a shame. She deserves it after this batting performance."

Dotty watched as Zivah opened the final over, striking the ball well and sending it running along the grass, past a fielder who threw herself at it but missed, before it reached the boundary rope for four.

"One three nine," commented Barry. Dotty presumed he was referring to the Coln Akeman Larks total run score.

The next ball Zivah struck only went a short distance, and Pip held up her hand.

"Why didn't they run?" asked Dotty, confused.

"Because Pip wants Zivah to remain facing the bowler, so she has a chance of hitting the next ball for six."

Zivah didn't, but she did hit another four, and after that, the two batters ran a desperate two.

"Pip is the perfect partner for Zivah. Two more balls," Barry said as he clasped and unclasped his hands in nervous excitement.

The next ball didn't quite reach the boundary, but Pip and Zivah ran an easy two, putting Zivah in position for the final ball.

She finished the innings with a commendable four.

Dotty glanced at the scoreboard as Zach updated it to one hundred and fifty-one, with ninety for batsman one.

"Well done, Zivah," Barry said, turning back into the pavilion. "And the whole team," he added, picking up one of the glasses he'd laid out on a white-clothed wooden trestle table.

As the spectators began walking towards the pavilion, Dotty returned to her position behind the tables which were groaning under the weight of all the food they'd prepared. She knew it wouldn't last long.

She and Keya had packed a separate tea for the players, officials, and helpers, so she didn't have to worry about the food running out as it nearly had at the first match.

"Hi, I thought I might help," said a breathless Gilly as she pushed through the gathering crowd and squeezed behind the food tables next to Dotty.

"Lovely flowers," she said, eyeing the vase of peonies. Their large blooms were in shades of pink and white, with rounded petals opening up in neat layers.

"And here we go," said Dotty as if a race was about to start.

A relatively orderly queue formed as people picked up paper plates and helped themselves, but soon hands were reaching here and there, and Dotty and Gilly had to work quickly to replenish empty serving dishes.

"I'm sorry, that was the last of the chicken skewers," Dotty apologised to an elderly man leaning on a cane.

"At least the rush is over," she said, turning to Gilly. "Do we know how the match is going?"

"Bryonie took an early wicket, but the two batters have been in for a while now. Sujin needs to do something to break up the partnership," replied Barry.

"He's putting Bernadette on to bowl," called a woman standing in the doorway, holding a paper plate of food.

"That'll certainly make them think," Barry chuckled.

And it did. Two minutes later, a burst of applause rang out.

"Bernadette took a wicket!" the woman by the door called back. "I've no idea how. I was sure the ball was going wide."

Play continued, and Dotty was able to watch some of the match while keeping an eye on the food and serving the few remaining spectators who wandered over to the pavilion.

Gilly jumped around excitedly when Olivia, squatting behind the wickets and facing the batsman, caught a ball Clara had bowled. Olivia held it up and cried, "Howzat!"

At the other end, the umpire, wearing a white shirt and a wide-brimmed white hat, held up his finger.

The batswoman was out.

But as they went into the final over, The Hereford Hinds were only twelve runs behind the Coln Akeman Larks with one wicket remaining.

Zivah was bowling. Her first ball was straight, fast, and long, and the batsman pushed it away defensively.

Her second ball pitched short, and the batswoman stepped in to strike it, but there must have been an edge of spin on the ball. The batter twisted, lost her balance, and struck the ball high into the air.

"Mine!" called Mel, catching it easily.

"They've won! They've won!" shouted Gilly excitedly, her orange ringlets bouncing up and down.

"Well we won't be serving food and drinks at their next match," Barry commented dryly. "They're playing at the Cotswold Summer Cricket Festival."

"In the final," added Dotty.

She grinned. She'd never imagined they could go so far in the competition, especially in their first season with such a diverse group of players. It might be slim, but they now had a chance to be the first winners of the Three Counties Ladies' Cricket Cup.

CHAPTER EIGHT

KEYA

The cricket pavilion at Coln Akeman was buzzing after the match, and so was Keya.

She still couldn't believe they'd won.

"You were definitely the player of the match," she said, enthusiastically hugging her sister, Zivah.

"The new kit really helped," Zivah replied, giving her husband Aadi a warm look. He was standing beside her, holding their young son, Kaami, who was waving a long cheese straw around in his small hand rather than eating it.

"Nonsense. You played brilliantly." Aadi leaned across and kissed Zivah on the cheek.

Kaami gurgled in delight and threw the cheese straw onto the floor.

Nearby, Zach and Mel turned towards them, and Zach said, "Don't forget Mel's winning catch."

"Of course not," Aadi said, raising his glass of ginger beer in acknowledgement.

"Oh, thank you, Zach," Mel said, touching his arm as she openly flirted with him. Leaning in closer, she lowered her voice in a conspiratorial tone and said, "We're going out tonight to celebrate, aren't we, Zach?"

From where Keya was standing, she could see Dotty nearby,

clearing empty paper plates and dropping them into a black dustbin bag. Although her friend kept her head down, Keya noticed her ears turn pink. She'd definitely heard Mel.

Zach cleared his throat. "I thought we all might like to, after such a fabulous win."

Zivah gave him a regretful smile. "We need to take Kaami home, and Aadi has work in the morning. But I hope you all have a wonderful time."

"Perhaps another day," Zach suggested.

"Oh, but I feel like partying tonight. And I have the evening off work. Why don't we go somewhere?" Mel pressed.

"Let me speak to Sujin and see what he thinks," Zach said diplomatically as he extracted himself from the group.

"And I'd better help Dotty tidy up," Keya added.

"We're off," said Zivah as Mel drifted away. The two sisters hugged, and Keya waved at Kaami as Aadi carried him out of the pavilion.

Nearby, Keya overheard a man say, "That was impressive play. It was not quite at Zivah's level, she was outstanding, but without you to support her, I doubt the team would have won."

Turning, she saw Pip and her partner.

Pip was dressed comfortably in a loose cream cotton blouse and beige linen shorts. She had swapped her trainers for a pair of canvas slip-on shoes. Although she was smaller than Keya, her arms and legs looked firm and muscular, and she gave Keya the impression that she was both strong and fit.

Her partner—Ned, that was his name—was certainly not athletic. He had a bookish look, being plumper and dressed in a light blue collared shirt, with the sleeves rolled up, and a pair of grey trousers.

Keya crossed to them and said, "Well played. Did you enjoy the match? Was it your first?"

"I... um..." Pip mumbled.

Ned interjected, "I was just telling her how well she did. She's not like your sister, but she contributed to your win."

"She certainly did," Keya replied, "and I hope you'll join us for the final at the Cotswold Summer Cricket Festival."

"I'm not sure..." Pip began, but her voice trailed off as she saw the disappointed look on Ned's face. "Let's see," she said smiling slowly at Keya.

But as Keya walked away, she reflected that Pip had looked sad, almost dejected when she'd looked at her.

Keya forgot about Pip as she saw Dotty with another black dustbin bag and asked, "What can I do to help?"

"Can you place all the leftover sandwiches on one plate and the cakes and bakes on another so people can still pick at them? And then tidy the dishes and containers away? Do we know how long people will stay? My head is starting to thump."

Keya had forgotten about Dotty's condition, and her cheeks coloured as she replied guiltily, "You shouldn't be doing this. I can get the team to help clear away."

"But what about…" Dotty's words trailed off as she glanced at Zach, and then searched the room for someone else. Was she looking for Mel?

"Zach suggested a celebratory evening, but I'm not sure it's going to happen. Most people have work tomorrow. Some of the players will probably go to the pub for a few drinks, but you don't need to."

"But…" Dotty began.

Keya lowered her voice, and her tone was reassuring as she said, "Zach is not going to disappear off with Mel tonight. I know I said you needed to be more proactive, but not today. You're tired and still feeling the effects of concussion."

Dotty smiled at her in relief.

"Hello, ladies," said Zach cheerfully as he approached. "A few of us were thinking about going to the pub for a drink to celebrate our win. Are you coming?"

"We need to tidy up here," Keya responded before Dotty could. "And Dotty is exhausted from working all day, and her head is sore."

"Oh gosh, I'd forgotten about that in the excitement of the match." Zach's expression shifted to one of concern and protectiveness as he looked at Dotty. "Look, why don't I join the team for a drink and then come back to yours to watch a film? I can grab a pizza or fish and chips in Fairford for supper. How does that sound?"

Dotty began, "There's no …" but Keya swiftly kicked her shins and shot her a meaningful look.

Dotty turned to her, momentarily taken aback, but then realisation dawned. Her expression shifted, and her eyes narrowed slightly, focusing on something—or someone—behind Keya.

"Actually, that sounds wonderful," she said lightly. "After I've finished clearing up, I think I'll go home for a long bath. What film do you fancy watching?"

As she and Zach discussed movies, Keya turned and saw Mel watching them.

Keya straightened her shoulders and smiled to herself. She was proud of her friend for standing her ground, and for not only accepting Zach's suggestion but purposefully discussing the evening's plans.

It was a start.

CHAPTER NINE

DOTTY

The following Sunday dawned warm and bright. Dotty pulled back the curtains in one of the spare bedrooms at Zach's house and looked out over the small orchard. Even the old twisted apple trees, which were bare when Zach had moved into this house on the edge of the Cotswold town of Burford, were thick with glossy leaves. And the small green apples beginning to form meant there would be plenty to pick in the Autumn if Zach was still living in the house.

Tap, tap.

"I'm up," Dotty called, answering Zach's enquiring knock on her door.

"Tea," said Zach as he entered the room carrying two mugs. He handed Dotty hers and then looked out of the window and said, "I can't wait to try the cherries. Are you sure we can't eat them yet? They look ready."

"Aunt Beanie said to wait. They need to be plumper and a deeper … well, cherry colour." Dotty smiled at Zach.

Returning the gesture he said, "Thank you for driving yesterday. You didn't find the beer festival too dull, did you?"

Dotty considered her response. She wanted to be truthful, without disappointing Zach, and if they were to spend time together she knew she had to both maintain her independence and make compromises.

"Drinking beer isn't really my thing, but I enjoyed watching you try different ones. Many of them have really strange names." Her smile broadened. "And some of the brewers had some interesting stories. I do like supporting local enterprises."

"And it was pleasant sitting out last tonight and listening to the band?"

"Oh, yes, I loved that. And my seafood paella. And you enjoyed your lamb koftas?"

"They were excellent. I could really taste the cumin and coriander which went so well with the tzatziki." He sipped his coffee and then added. "And all this talk of food has made me hungry. Let's get ourselves sorted and meet downstairs for breakfast. We better not hang around as I calculated we need to leave in an hour."

Zach left and Dotty continued to sip her tea as she stared out over the orchard, feeling as warm and content as the sunshine outside. And she was looking forward to the cricket tournament today, particularly as she didn't have to play.

Dotty threaded the string of her player's badge through a buttonhole of her short, pale yellow fitted jacket before pulling out her sunglasses.

"This is great," Zach said, securing his own badge to the lapel of his new navy blazer. He had bought one for himself and another for Sujin, both embroidered with Coln Akeman Larks and the image of a lark on the breast pocket.

"It means we not only get to watch our team's match from the players pavilion but also have access to the VIP stand for the county match afterwards. That's if you want to stay?" He glanced over at Dotty.

"Of course, and it is such a lovely day." She tilted her head towards the sun.

"It might even get too hot," warned Zach.

"I have my hat," she replied, holding up the wide brimmed straw one she was carrying.

"Dotty and Zach," called a loud, slightly pretentious voice.

They turned towards it, and Dotty forced a smile as they walked forward to meet Adrian Cartwright, Deputy Headmaster of Ashcombe Manor School, which was hosting the cricket festival.

"How are you both?" greeted Adrian jovially. "And the women's team you sponsor, they're in the final this morning, aren't they? It's a generous gesture to support minority sports. I don't think I'll be watching the game myself, but still, reaching the final is an impressive feat for a group of ladies."

Zach must have caught the derisory note in Adrian's statement as he replied, "It certainly is in our first season, but I think one or two of the players could give the professionals a run for their money."

"Run for their money," laughed Adrian. "Great pun." But the laughter died as he watched the tall figure of Gifford Rivers stride easily past them. Hurrying to keep up with him was a middle-aged woman wearing a smart black blazer with a yellow insignia on the front.

"So Gifford's in with Harriet Wintle is he? He always was a ladies' man. No wonder he gets his own way," Adrian muttered. "Well, nearly always." And then he turned without saying another word to Dotty and Zach and raised his arm as he called out, "Cliff. Not there."

He marched away towards the rich brown-skinned groundsman Dotty had seen working when they'd been preparing for the auction. Cliff, the groundsman, removed his white hat and scratched at his short white hair as Adrian approached him.

Nearby, Gifford and the smartly dressed lady had stopped to talk.

As Dotty and Zach approached them at a leisurely pace Gifford looked across and grinned. "I just love the vintage cricket bat I bought at your auction. I've actually put it on display in the members pavilion today."

Zach, who was ever the businessman, replied, "That's great. And I hope you'll attend some of our auctions in the future. We might have more themed ones, or at least themed sections."

The important-looking lady in the black blazer cleared her throat. Dotty noticed that the embroidered emblem on her jacket matched the one printed on the front of the day's programme, a copy of which she was carrying.

Without faltering, Gifford said, "Can I introduce you to Harriet Wintle, the newest member of the Gloucestershire County Cricket board, and the reason the Three Counties Ladies' Cricket Cup is taking place."

"Harriet," Gifford continued, "Zach and Dotty run Akemans auction house which is one of the sponsors of the Coln Akeman Larks."

"How wonderful. And thank you for your support," Harriet said, smiling.

"Dotty was in the team," Zach said, "until she was injured recently."

"Oh, I'm so sorry you're missing out on the final. But you'll have a wonderful view from the players pavilion," said Harriet, noting Dotty's badge. "And you managed to find a replacement?"

"Yes," Zach replied. "Although she's hardly had any practice. We roped her in because she happened to be walking her dog the evening Dotty was injured."

"That's the spirit," Harriet responded, glancing at her watch. "It's lovely to meet you both," she said distractedly to Zach and Dotty. "Gifford?"

The two of them walked away.

Dotty wondered what her former teammates were doing and then she noticed the stocky bespectacled figure of Ned and, with him, the smaller Pip, whose head and most of her face appeared to be hidden by a large baseball cap.

"I can't understand how your trainers were missing. It's not as if Willow took them. Or perhaps he did. But both of them? And then to find them placed neatly behind the washing machine? Anyway, don't let that bother you now. You have the match to look forward to and isn't this exciting?"

Ned certainly appeared impressed as his gaze swept round the cricket ground.

Ashcombe Manor had done an excellent job. The large marquee where Akemans had held their auction at the end of June had been replaced by other small tents of varying shapes and sizes, arranged in a large circle around the cricket field and interspersed with stands of temporary seating.

But Pip must be nervous as she appeared unaware of her surroundings, keeping her head bowed and her shoulders slumped. Her steps were short shuffles and not the usual confident strides Dotty was used to seeing.

Ned carried her navy kit bag and led her away to the left.

"I think the changing rooms and players pavilion are this way," Zach said. "Shall we go and see them? Sujin might need you to calm Keya down."

They found Sujin standing outside a larger version of Coln Akeman's wooden white-washed pavilion. This one was two storeys high, with a balcony running the length of the first floor, and tables and chairs set out behind a white picket fence at ground level.

"So, Sujin, your team has had quite the journey to the final. But some critics are saying the team has been a bit lucky with the competition they've faced. Do you think your team is truly ready for the pressure of the final, or are they still a bit green?" asked a woman Dotty thought she recognised.

"That's Clare Savage, the sports journalist," whispered Zach. "I've been listening to her podcast. It's very entertaining. She doesn't hold her punches when it comes to interviewing her guests."

Dotty wondered if that meant she was blunt, or even bordered on being on rude. She certainly seemed to be invading Sujin's space, leaning forward and staring intently at him as he answered her question calmly and politely.

"I'd say both teams in the final have earned their place, Clare. We've worked hard all season, and luck plays a small part, but what really matters is the effort and commitment the players have shown. I believe in my team's abilities, and we are prepared for the final, just as we have been for every match leading up to it."

Clare pressed on. "Your team has some talented players, but a lot of them are still pretty inexperienced at this level of competition. Do you worry that they might crack under the pressure of the final?"

"I think every player has potential, and they've all shown tremendous growth over the season. The key to handling pressure is staying focused and trusting the process we've built together. I don't think they'll crack. They've proven themselves time and time again. And now, if you'll excuse me?"

Sujin dipped his head and left Clare as she was about to ask him another question. He joined Dotty and Zach.

"That journalist is right about one thing. The cracks are starting to show. Keya is both exuberant and a bag of nerves. And Zivah called and said she would be late because Kaami was sick this morning. And I haven't seen Pip."

"We have," Zach said. "And don't worry, Zivah will be here. It's still" – he checked his brown leather-strapped wristwatch – "fifty minutes until play starts. Why doesn't Dotty go and speak to Keya and see if she can calm her down?"

"Excellent idea," Sujin replied, looking relieved. He took a deep breath and continued, "And I should encourage those who've already changed to come out for a warm-up and practice. We need to settle the nerves." He gave them a wry smile. "Mine as much as anyone's."

CHAPTER TEN

KEYA

Where was her other white sock?

Keya rooted around in her pink sports bag until she found it, hiding at the bottom under her yellow towel.

Her hands shook as she sat down to pull on both socks.

"I remember…" began Aunt Beanie, but her reminiscence was cut short by Tani Hargreaves's dramatic entrance as she gushed, "I've just seen Gifford Rivers, and he's even more gorgeous in the flesh!"

"Is Zach here?" Mel enquired.

"He's coming with Dotty," Keya replied pointedly. "They were at the Cotswold Beer Festival together yesterday."

"Oh, I wanted to go to that, but Barry made me work a double shift since I'm off today."

"My mum said that was to stop you drinking too much at the festival and feeling rubbish today," Bryonie piped up.

"What?" Mel looked indignant.

"He was probably right," joked Tani. "Can you imagine nursing a hangover in this heat?"

"We should all drink plenty of water," Marion instructed.

"But what if I need a pee in the middle of the match?" Olivia asked. "Talking of which, I need one now."

"It's just the nerves," Marion called after her.

"I certainly feel nervous," admitted Clara, who was sitting beside Keya, tying her shoelaces "But it's so exciting, isn't it? Our first season, and here we are playing in front of a large crowd. Have you seen all the grandstands?"

"Those are for the county match this afternoon. I don't think we'll have a large crowd," Aunt Beanie remarked.

"Oh, I do hope someone comes to watch us," Mel said, sounding disappointed.

"Ready!" called Keya, jumping up. Then she stopped and looked round. "Where are Pip and Zivah? They have to come. We can't rely on Dotty again, not for the final."

"We're here," she heard Ned reply as Pip was propelled into the women's changing room. "And here's your bag," Ned called after her as a navy sports bag skimmed along the floor. "I'll be waiting outside if you need me."

Marion approached Pip, who stood frozen just inside the doorway. "Don't worry, we're all nervous. But there are no expectations on you. You've only had one match and a few practices. Please, just try to enjoy it."

Pip removed her hat and smiled gratefully at Marion, but she looked very pale.

"It'll be better once we start playing," Aunt Beanie declared as she pulled on her light green and red diamond-patterned 'lucky' socks.

"Do you think she'll be allowed to wear those for the final?" whispered Clara, looking up at Keya.

"Would you try to take them off her?"

Clara grinned.

There was a rap on the changing room door, which stood ajar, and Sujin called, "Is anyone ready to practice?"

"Yes, definitely," Keya called, dashing out of the changing room. "Are the other team here?" she asked as she joined Sujin outside. "What do they look like? And have you heard from Zivah? She hasn't arrived, and…"

Sujin held up his hand. "Everything's under control. Zivah is on her way. But Dotty is here. Why don't you chat to her while I hurry up the rest of the team?"

"Hiya," Keya greeted Dotty. "Isn't this exciting? Oh, sorry. I mean, it is exciting, but are you disappointed to be missing out?"

"Oh no," Dotty smiled. "I'll be right where I want to be. Watching safely from the sidelines."

"Do you know why Zivah's late?" Keya asked in a concerned voice.

"I think Kaami was a little under the weather this morning. But she'll be here. Don't worry."

Other members of the team slowly appeared.

Mel made a beeline for Zach.

Keya raised her voice and asked, "And how was the beer festival yesterday? Did you two have fun?"

"I wasn't bothered about the drinking, but I enjoyed talking to the brewers. And listening to the band in the evening was fun." She glanced across at Zach, and a cloud passed over her face.

"It was a great day," Zach said, smiling at Dotty and Keya.

Dotty brightened as Mel looked sulky.

"Everybody ready for the match?" Adrian Cartwright asked as he joined them.

"Nearly," Ned replied. "You're the deputy head here, aren't you? I'm Ned Pritchard. I recently joined Farmor's in Fairford as the head of English."

"They have nice grounds for a state school, but nothing like ours. Would you like me to show you around? We're always on the lookout for talented teachers."

"That would be great. Thank you." Turning to Sujin, Ned said, "Can you let Pip know I've just gone for a look around? I'll be back before the match starts."

"Of course."

Ned and Adrian walked away as Olivia and Pip appeared from the pavilion.

"Right, ladies. Time to practise," said Sujin, striding out after them.

"Sorry, I'm late," Zivah called as she jogged past them towards the pavilion.

"No rush. Take your time," Sujin replied after her, clearly relieved that she'd arrived in time.

CHAPTER ELEVEN

KEYA

Sujin asked Marion to take the toss, and even though she lost and the other side, the Evesham Eagles, opted to field, Marion returned to where the Coln Akeman Larks were warming up with a steady, confident stride and said encouragingly, "The team that loses the toss wins the match."

"I'm not sure that's a saying," grumbled Aunt Beanie. "I'd rather be fielding first rather than hanging around in the pavilion, waiting to go out to bat."

Keya glanced at the older woman and, for the first time, noticed the flicker of nerves as Aunt Beanie's hand ran down her loose white shorts.

And if steadfast Aunt Beanie was nervous… Keya felt her stomach flutter.

Dotty and Zach were standing on the other side of the perimeter rail, chatting to Ned.

Keya rushed over and asked, "Dotty, will you sit with me? My nerves are all a jitter."

"Of course," Dotty replied, linking her arm through Keya's as they walked towards the front of the pavilion. The Coln Akeman Larks had based themselves on the left-hand side and the Evesham Eagles on the right, and both teams were shaded from the sun by the overhang of the first-floor balcony.

The rest of the team filed off the field and, as they approached the white-painted boundary, Cliff, the groundsman, removed his hat, scratched his head, and enquired, "Philippa Lawson?"

Nobody responded.

Pip was still very pale as she sat down next to Ned.

He patted her leg encouragingly.

Sujin said, "I've changed the usual batting order. Clara and Marion, you'll go out first." As they reached for pairs of long white batting pads, he continued, "You two are both level-headed. Don't try any clever shots. Just defend, stay in, and wear down their best bowlers."

Looking at the rest of the team, he continued, "If they stay in for several overs, we'll send Zivah out at number three, but I want her to watch the play first. If there's a quick wicket, you can go out, Keya."

"Me?" Keya squawked.

"Yes. Just remember what we've practised. Keep the face of your bat pointing down and step into the shots, using the pace of the bowler to send the ball running along the ground."

Keya gripped Dotty's hand nervously, before she started to search the pile of pads for the ones she preferred.

Zivah calmly strapped on her own smart-looking pads before weighing her bat in her hand. She glanced out over the field as the Evesham Eagles tossed the ball between themselves. Their players moved into position around the pitch, waiting for the first Coln Akeman batswomen.

"Ready?" Sujin asked as Clara re-tied her shoelace.

"As I'll ever be," replied Marion stoically.

"I think so," Clara said with a nervous smile. They picked up their bats and strode onto the pitch as the commentator announced, "And here are the first of the Coln Akeman players. I don't have a batting order, so if someone could let me know who they are?"

"I'll do that," volunteered Zach as he stood up, looking relieved as he left Mel sitting in the seat beside him.

Play began, and the first two bowlers for the Evesham Eagles bowled fast and straight.

"Good shot, Marion!" Sujin called as she stepped neatly forward and pushed the ball away. It skimmed across the smooth grass, and Marion and Clara claimed a single run.

Clara was less confident, but she kept her bat down, moving it cautiously as the balls flew towards her. But at the start of the third over, one ball skidded past her and clipped the right-hand stump. The umpire, dressed in a traditional white jacket, raised his finger. Clara was out.

Sujin looked between Keya and Zivah, weighing up his options.

The bowling was fast, and Keya noticed Zivah jiggling her right leg up and down nervously.

"I'll go in," Keya volunteered, jumping up. "And take some of the flak."

Relieved, Sujin said, "Thank you." Then he added, "You're more than ready for this. Just remember what I said when we practised in the garden last night. Short, downward movements. No wild strokes. This is about staying the course, not racking up a quick succession of fours and sixes only to get caught out."

"Good luck," Dotty encouraged her. "I know you can do this. Just step into the ball, not back."

Keya smiled nervously at Sujin, picked up her bat, and walked out onto the pitch. At first, her steps were small and hesitant, but then she heard clapping.

Looking around, she realised there were far more people watching than she had expected. The stands were only partly full, but in the areas between and in front of the tents, people were sitting down or leaning against the perimeter rail.

People who were there to see her. To watch her team, which hadn't even existed four months ago.

Lifting her head, she gripped the handle of her bat with determination and strode forward with purpose.

"Is this the one?" whispered a fielder as she passed.

"I think so. Let's move out."

They thought she was Zivah.

But if her sister could play with such poise and skill, why couldn't she? Sujin was right. She was ready for this. She could do it.

"OK?" said Marion, walking up to meet her.

"Actually, yes, I am. What's the plan?"

"We're just aiming for a few singles and staying in, so they use up overs with their best bowlers. The one from the pavilion end is just fast. If you can read her deliveries and knock them away, you'll be fine. But watch out for the other bowler. The ball that got Clara out had a slight spin, but she mostly targets the right side. You're facing her first, so be careful."

Keya walked steadily to her crease, the area she would bat from. This was always the most vulnerable time for a new batter. But she only had to face one ball before the change of over, which also meant a change of ends. Then Marion would be facing the bowling.

One ball.

Standing sideways to the wicket, she looked forwards, slowing her breathing. Her hands shook. She placed the bat's end on the ground, flexed her fingers, then lifted it again. Don't grip too tightly. Keep it just clear of the ground, angled slightly downward. Don't rush. Let the ball come to her.

The bowler ran in quickly and released the ball, but Keya saw it clearly. Marion was right. She was bowling to the right. Keya stepped across, pushed her bat forward, followed through with a downward stroke, and sent the ball whizzing across the ground between two fielders.

"Run!" Marion called.

And Keya did.

"And another!" Marion instructed.

Panting slightly, Keya sprinted back to her starting position. She always felt awkward in her collection of batting pads, thick gloves, and visored helmet, but she was getting used to running in them.

"Over," called the umpire.

"An excellent opening shot from Coln Akeman Lark's batter, Keya Varma, taking her team to twenty-one for one after three overs."

Marion met Keya in the middle of the pitch. How long could they keep their partnership going?

CHAPTER TWELVE

KEYA

The final of the Three Counties Ladies' Cricket Cup was well underway, with Coln Akeman Larks steadying themselves at the crease.

"That was great," Marion said, nodding her green-helmeted head. "But don't take any chances. We're just laying the groundwork before your sister steps in."

Keya felt elated after her first shot but took a deep breath. Marion was right. Zivah was the star of the show. She just needed to set things up for her.

For the next two overs, Keya held her defensive stance and, between them, she and Marion steadily picked up singles or pairs of runs.

A new bowler stepped up for the sixth over. Without a run-up, she sent a spinning ball towards Keya, who sidestepped and let it pass. It skimmed dangerously close to her wicket. That was lucky.

She connected with the next ball, and she and Marion ran a single, putting Marion on strike.

But Keya watched in dismay as Marion, about to hit the ball one way, adjusted her footing at the last moment, reacting to the bounce. Her bat connected with the ball, but instead of a controlled shot, the ball looped into the air. The wicketkeeper sprinted forward and caught it cleanly.

Marion was out.

"Unlucky," Keya murmured as her partner passed.

Marion managed a small smile. "Good luck." Then, with purposeful strides, she walked off the pitch.

Zivah was next. She looked so professional and composed as she strode onto the pitch, pulling on her gloves and tucking her bat under her arm with ease.

"Come on, girls!" shouted a familiar voice.

Surprised, Keya turned towards the closest boundary. Her mother, wearing a bright red sari, waved at her.

"Keep going," called her usually reserved father. "We're so proud of you both."

A lump rose in Keya's throat as she turned to greet her sister.

"Marion's told me what to expect, and I've been discussing the bowlers with Sujin," Zivah said, all business, as Keya quickly removed a glove and dabbed at her eye.

"Are you okay?" Zivah asked.

"Just the sun," Keya lied, gulping as she tried to steady herself. She was playing alongside her sister. In the finals of the Ladies' Cricket Tournament. The thought overwhelmed her for a moment, but as she walked back to her crease, she muttered under her breath, "Stay calm. Support Zivah."

And that's exactly what she did.

Zivah didn't let the spinning ball catch her out. Instead, she stepped into the shot and whisked it away before it had time to bounce.

They ran two runs.

Then Zivah went for the boundary.

She struck a bouncing four, then ran two more to finish the over.

"And a fantastic start by top-scoring batswoman Zivah Patel to put the Coln Akeman Larks onto fifty runs. It's fifty for two, with sisters Keya and Zivah batting."

Keya was starting to tire. Zivah, who was getting fewer balls past the excellent fielders, made sure they ran for every single, which meant

Keya kept facing the bowlers. Concentrating on the different styles of bowling was exhausting.

In the ninth over Keya misjudged a spin. The ball curved behind her and knocked off the bails. She was out.

"Sorry, sis," she said.

"Why? Between us, we've taken the score to eighty-three, and you've hit a personal best. Look. twenty-eight runs!" Zivah stared at the scoreboard.

"Good luck," Keya said as she walked off the pitch.

"Brilliant," Sujin said as she stepped onto the sidelines, giving her a quick, proud hug. "You've set things up perfectly. Now we just need the others to back up Zivah."

But they didn't.

Aunt Beanie ignored the advice to play sensibly. She hit the ball wildly and, on her second shot, it was caught just in front of the boundary.

"They were lucky," she muttered as she returned to the pavilion.

Georgina Carey lasted a little longer and batted well, but a fast-paced delivery caught her off guard, and she was out.

Mel, Tani, Olivia, and Bryonie tried hard, but they were outclassed by the opposition.

"And the Coln Akeman batting is collapsing after such a promising start," reported the commentator.

The score was ninety-six for nine after thirteen overs.

Sujin turned to Pip, who was standing up, clutching her cricket bat. "I'm sorry to put you in this position," he said. "We still have over six overs, so we need you to stay in and support Zivah for as long as possible. Keep calm, play steadily, and don't take unnecessary risks. We're not expecting you to rack up runs, but we do need to set a high enough target. Otherwise, this could turn into a very one-sided match."

Pip bit her lip and glanced at her teammates before walking steadily onto the pitch.

"And now, please welcome the final player for the Coln Akeman Larks. Pip Lawton."

Pip flinched slightly when the commentator announced her name, but as cheers and shouts of encouragement echoed around the ground, she paused. Then she turned in a slow circle, taking it all in.

"That's a good idea," said Sujin, leaning against the railing.

Keya, who was sitting with Dotty, asked, "What is?"

"She's finding her bearings. I bet it's daunting, walking out there. And there are even more people watching now."

"It is," Keya agreed, remembering her own experience. But also exhilarating.

As Pip approached Zivah, her entire demeanour shifted. She carried herself with quiet confidence, meeting Zivah's gaze steadily before tapping her bat against the dry, brown pitch.

She faced the bowler. Stepping forward early, she drove the ball away for two runs.

"Fabulous start. Well done, Pip," shouted Sujin. Then turning to Ned, he said, "She looks really comfortable out there. It's amazing what a match and a couple of training sessions can do."

Ned smiled proudly as Pip faced the bowler again.

Zach joined Keya and Dotty. "Fingers crossed," he said. "Pip's playing what I think Sujin would call a solid game."

Sujin gave a brief nod but kept his attention on the pitch, his fingers drumming against the white railing.

Zivah was being more cautious now, opting for singles and steady play over risky boundary shots. But between her and Pip, they were inching the score higher.

"They've added forty-eight runs between them, which is brilliant," Sujin said. "That takes us to one hundred and forty-four. Let's see if they can push it past one hundred and fifty in the final over."

Zivah smashed the next ball for six.

Keya jumped up, clapping. "That's one hundred and fifty!"

"And sixty-six for Zivah," added Sujin, joining in the applause.

As the commentators praised Zivah's performance, she raised her bat in acknowledgement, smiling briefly before settling back at the crease.

The next ball was bowled short, and she could only drive it a short distance.

"Run!" called Pip, already halfway down the pitch.

"Pip's on strike," Ned said excitedly.

Pip hit a clean four, driving the ball past the shortest boundary. Then she took a single, putting Zivah back on strike.

Zivah struck a four with her next shot.

"Last ball," said Keya. She was on edge. Could Zivah finish with another six?

She certainly tried. The ball was bowled short, and she lifted it high into the air.

Would it clear the boundary? Keya held her breath as she watched it fall.

"Oh no, it's going to land short," Sujin said.

"And be caught," Zach said.

A fielder was already in position and took the catch with ease.

Lively music blared from the speakers as the players on the pitch acknowledged the applause.

There were loud cheers as Zivah and Pip walked proudly back to the pavilion.

The music faded, and the commentator announced, "The final score for the Coln Akeman Larks is one hundred and sixty. The highest scorer is Zivah Patel, followed by strong performances from Pip Lawton—twenty-five not out—and Zivah's sister, Keya, on twenty-eight. We'll take a short break before returning for the second innings." Softer, classical music played across the ground.

Sujin turned to the team. "Now the hard work really begins," he said. "We're fielding."

CHAPTER THIRTEEN

DOTTY

Dotty had found watching her former teammates bat both exhilarating and nerve-wracking. She was so proud of her colleagues, Marion and Clara, for their commendable performance opening the batting. How daunting must it have been for them to walk out onto this ground? With the commentators, the music, and the growing crowd, it was a far cry from their pleasant village cricket field.

Zivah had played sensibly, working hard to keep the Coln Akeman Larks' chances alive, even as she lost a steady stream of batting partners. But it was her final partnership with Pip that had truly turned the game. And what a revelation Pip had been. Dotty had thought she had the athletic, sporty look about her, but to pick up cricket so quickly? Even after numerous practices and several matches, Dotty knew she could never bat like that.

Zach handed her a cup of tea in a cardboard cup and sat down.

"Thank you. And wasn't Keya brilliant today? She was so chuffed with her batting, and so she should be."

"I always knew there was a steely core beneath her sometimes-over-exuberant exterior. Otherwise, I couldn't see how she'd been so successful in her job," Zach reflected.

"Her intuition is usually spot on, and once she suspects something isn't right, she pulls together a group of people to help prove it. I think that's why she enjoys cricket so much. She likes the team element."

"Whereas you're more of a lone wolf," Zach teased.

Dotty considered his words before replying, "I suppose I do prefer working things out on my own. Probably because I didn't have the chance to earlier in life. I love discussing things with you, Keya, Aunt Beanie, or Norman, but I like time and space to think things through."

"Here come our ladies," Zach said as the Coln Akeman Larks emerged from the players' pavilion and spilled onto the pitch.

"Don't they look smart in their new kit?" Zach added, straightening the lapels on his blazer.

Dotty smiled. He'd arranged for the entire team to wear new shirts with Akemans printed on the back, along with an image of a waterwheel to represent Keya's cafe.

"Now I know why you didn't want the company name on the front. Nobody would see it since the spectators are always looking at the players' backs."

"It was actually a tip from Sujin," Zach admitted. "But you're right. They all look great. Like a proper team."

Aunt Beanie settled herself closest to the boundary, her long white hair held back by a sunflower yellow scarf. Nearly professional, thought Dotty, glancing at the enormous bow Aunt Beanie had tied on the side of her head, and remembering her 'lucky' socks.

Olivia squatted behind one of the wickets, and Georgina, who appeared to be opening the bowling, gracefully threw the ball to her.

"Sorry I left you for the first half of the match, but it was interesting speaking to the commentary team, and I met Gifford Rivers again," Zach said. "He showed me round the members' pavilion. It's very plush in there. You'd love all the fresh flowers, and they were serving tasty cakes and biscuits alongside tea and coffee. I've never had Battenberg cake before, and Gifford suggested I bring you a piece."

Zach reached into his pocket and removed a white paper napkin, which he passed to Dotty. She took it and pulled back the tissue to reveal a square piece of cake surrounded by a thin layer of marzipan. The light sponge cake was famed for its checked pattern, with two squares of pink cake and two of yellow. A layer of jam separated the quarters.

"Thank you," Dotty said as she lifted the cake to her mouth. It was delicious and perfect with her cup of tea.

The crowd applauded as the two opening batswomen for the Evesham Eagles walked steadily onto the pitch.

"They look formidable," Zach commented. "While I was in the members' tent, I saw the cricket bat Gifford acquired from us. He's put it in an open frame and hung it from the side of the tent. Several people were admiring it and asking where he'd bought it, so he introduced me to them. When Sujin suggested we sponsor a ladies' cricket team, I had no idea how good it would be for business."

"I saw that bat too when Adrian Cartwright showed me around," said another voice from behind them. Dotty turned to see Ned.

"Do you hold regular auctions? We're looking for a few quality pieces of furniture," he added.

"Every month," Zach replied enthusiastically. "And because last month's sale was mostly smaller pieces, there'll be a lot of furniture in the one we're holding at the end of this month."

They'd moved the auction back a week from their usual schedule to give themselves extra time to prepare the premises. It looked as if they would need to use the former storerooms rather than the main auction house, which was still covered in scaffolding.

On the field, Georgina ran up to the crease and released the ball. The batter made contact but only succeeded in pushing it back to Georgina.

"I also met Clare Savage," Zach continued.

"Good ball," Sujin remarked, watching Georgina's second ball pass the batswoman. Olivia stopped it and threw it back to Georgina.

"I'm not sure I'm such a fan of hers now," admitted Zach.

"Who? Clare Savage?" Sujin asked, turning round.

"Yes, she started interrogating me about our players. She couldn't believe Zivah hasn't played before this season."

"She's after dirt. That's what her column and podcasts thrive on. But she won't find any in our sleepy village team. Oh no!" groaned Sujin, returning to the cricket as the opposition hit the ball for four.

"There are no ringers in our team," Zach said as they continued watching the play.

Dotty had been relaxed at first, but as the score climbed past one hundred, she started feeling tense for her former teammates.

When the score rose to one hundred and thirty-one, and one of the batters acknowledged the applause from the crowd for reaching her half-century, Sujin muttered, "If we don't get her out in the next few balls, we're finished. They still have four overs to play."

On the field, Pip approached Marion, whom Sujin had appointed captain, and they spoke intensely for several minutes until the umpire called to them.

"What do you think that was about?" Dotty asked Zach.

"I've no idea. But perhaps Pip's also realised they need to get that player out. Maybe she suggested someone else bowl."

"I hope it's not Aunt Beanie. Her balls catch people out, but at this level…"

"I'll have you know, I've already taken a wicket," Aunt Beanie called across from just inside the boundary, where she was fielding and must have heard them. Dotty felt her cheeks redden.

"Pip's going to bowl," Sujin said in surprise as the small but compact player caught the ball and walked away from the pitch. She kept walking.

"What is she doing?" asked Dotty.

"I think that's her run-up," Sujin replied. "Look, she's marking the pitch with her foot. But how does she know about doing that? And why run so far? In fact, why has Marion let her bowl at this crucial time?"

"Perhaps she felt she'd run out of options," Dotty suggested.

"I'm sure my Pip won't let you down. She's a formidable tennis player. How different can cricket be?" Ned asked, sounding both proud and slightly nervous.

Dotty held her breath as Pip ran in. She was almost sprinting when she hopped to a stop and released the ball. It sped straight at the batter, who held her bat helplessly in front of her. Pip dived forward to catch the ball when it bounced off the player's bat, but just missed it.

"Wow. That was amazing," said Sujin. "It'll certainly have shaken the opposition."

And indeed it had. Two balls later, one of Pip's fast balls smashed through the stumps of the player who had recently celebrated her half-century.

"She's got her out!" cried Sujin, thumping the air.

Dotty smiled. He really cared about cricket and his team.

Pip also bowled out the player's replacement with the last ball of the over.

"Bernadette," Marion called.

"See? My services are needed," Aunt Beanie called before jogging towards the centre of the field.

Her enthusiasm paid off and she also took a wicket before handing the ball back to Pip.

"One more wicket," muttered Sujin under his breath. The scoreboard read one hundred and forty-one for nine.

Pip repeated her excellent bowling performance.

Marion, after a discussion with Zivah, had moved several fielders closer to the batswoman. Whether to crowd and panic her or to catch shorter hits, Dotty wasn't sure.

Pip bowled her first ball. The batter reached out to protect her wicket and connected. The speed of the ball sent it racing over the ground and the batters ran for two.

"Come on," murmured Sujin tensely.

Pip's second ball whizzed past the wicket, and Olivia threw herself sideways to stop it.

The tension was mounting.

Pip ran in but steadied as she reached the wicket. She released a slower ball, but it bounced high in front of the batswoman, who tried to hit it. She did, but the ball went high.

"Mine," Mel called, positioning herself under the ball and catching it with ease.

The umpire held up his finger.

"We've won!" exclaimed Sujin before rushing onto the field.

"That was great play from Pip," Zach said, turning to a proud but slightly bemused Ned.

"I could never have played like that," Dotty said. "It's lucky I got injured and she joined the team."

"Are you sure she's never played before?" asked Zach brightly.

"I don't think so... not that I know of," Ned replied, but his voice cracked with uncertainty. He removed his glasses and rubbed his eyes.

Zach and Dotty turned back towards the field. Zach placed his arm around Dotty's shoulders and pulled her close.

"And there I was, thinking cricket was a man's game, and a boring one at that. But that was so exciting."

Dotty watched as the beaming Coln Akeman Larks congratulated each other.

Keya ran over to Dotty and Zach, exclaiming, "I can't believe it. We won! And I hope you have a team shirt too, as you'll have to join us for the prize-giving. After all, you're part of the team. We couldn't have done it without you."

"I'm afraid I don't," Dotty replied feeling disappointed.

Out of his blazer pocket, Zach removed a folded white polo shirt. "I have one right here."

"But what about my dress?" Dotty protested.

"Just pull it on over the top," Keya suggested.

Dotty removed her yellow jacket as the other players filed off the field, chatting animatedly. Pip, Zivah, and Marion stopped to speak with Sujin. As they did, Clare Savage marched across the grass and called out as she approached them, "Philippa Lawson, how does it feel to win at the Cotswold Summer Cricket Festival again?"

CHAPTER FOURTEEN

DOTTY

Dotty didn't pull on her Coln Akeman Larks' white team polo shirt.

Instead, she, and all the people sitting and standing nearby, stopped talking and turned to look towards the small group at the side of the cricket field.

Zivah bowed her head to talk to Marion and Pip, as Sujin walked purposefully towards Clare Savage.

Dotty heard Sujin ask, "What are you talking about? Who is Philippa Lawson?"

"Philippa!" called Gifford Rivers, jogging along the side of the pitch. "That was fabulous. You should never have left cricket."

Pip muttered something, and Marion gave her a sharp look. Then Pip said something to Zivah and Marion, both of whom froze, stunned expressions on their faces.

Pip smiled apologetically at them before stepping out to meet Gifford. He threw his arms around her, lifted her off her feet, and spun her around.

"I've missed you," Dotty heard him say.

Zach nudged her arm and indicated behind her with his head.

She looked round.

Ned was leaning forward, his mouth open as he stared at Pip. Then he blinked, shook his head, and stood up. "Excuse me," he said, but instead of walking towards Pip and Gifford, he headed away from the players' and supporters' area.

Aunt Beanie approached Dotty, Zach and Keya, her eyes wide and bright. "Can you believe it? Our little Pip Lawton is really Philippa Lawson."

"And who's she?" Zach asked, pulling at his chin.

"The once bright star of women's cricket, until she was beset by scandal and disappeared from the game. And here she is, in Coln Akeman, playing for our village team. Quite the comedown."

"I wonder if that's why she was reluctant to take my place," said Dotty thoughtfully.

"Because she felt village cricket was beneath her?" asked Aunt Beanie.

"No, because changing her surname from Lawton to Lawson and using a shortened version of her first name probably means she was doing her best to step away from the cricketing scene."

Dotty watched as Gifford let go of Pip, and Clare Savage strode purposefully towards her. A ripple of unease passed through Dotty. Had her injury, and the team's need for a last-minute substitute, dragged Pip back into a world she had deliberately left behind? And what had driven her away from it in the first place?

Pip turned towards Clare, positioning her feet shoulder-width apart as she faced her. Her posture was erect but guarded as she raised her chin and said, "Clare. It's good to see you. And to answer your question, it felt great to walk onto the pitch with the appreciative applause of the crowd. And to be part of a team who are really passionate about the game, and supportive and encouraging of each other."

Pip glanced at Zivah and Marion, and Sujin, who had rejoined them.

"I couldn't let them down when they needed me. Not after all the time and effort they've put into practising and preparing for the final. This might be their only chance of playing here and winning the cup, so yes. It feels fantastic."

Pip spoke the last words deliberately.

The two women obviously knew each other from the past, and

Dotty wondered if Pip was trying to take the sting out of any follow-up questions. And her words were gracious. But had returning to the game come at a cost? And had she taken a personal risk just to help the Coln Akeman Larks win the cup?

Zivah strode across, as Clare asked in a mischievous tone, "What about your husband? Does Adrian know you're here?"

Zivah placed her arm around Pip's shoulders and said, "Our team would like to celebrate their win now. We'll be happy to answer any questions you have about our performance. Later."

Pip smiled up at her appreciatively as the two women left the field.

Gifford, who was now standing close to Clare, said, "I can't wait for Adrian to find out Philippa is here. He was such a beast to her."

Clare turned and looked up at him as she replied, "You weren't much better. You're the real reason she disappeared off the face of the earth."

Clare turned and stalked away as Gifford's mouth fell open. He was clearly shocked by Clare's words, and surprised. Did Clare know something he didn't, or was she just delivering a final blow to make him feel bad?

At first, the Coln Akeman Larks were silent when Zivah and Pip entered the pavilion area. But then Zach jumped up, shouting, "Well played!" and began clapping.

Pip smiled gratefully and Zivah, in relief, did the same.

Dotty stood and joined Zach, also clapping. "You both played so well. You all did," she said, looking around at the team. She had to force the smile to remain on her face as Mel gave Zach a coy smile.

"Put your top on. You're one of the team too, and we have to celebrate," Keya instructed her, grabbing the white polo shirt Dotty had placed on the seat and pulling it over her head.

The two friends laughed as Dotty took over and smoothed the shirt down.

The lady Dotty had seen when they'd first arrived – Harriet someone – who was wearing a black Gloucestershire County Cricket blazer, approached them and said, "Congratulations, ladies. A wonderful effort and great for the sport and the Three Counties Cup. Everyone loves it when the underdogs win."

Olivia and Bryonie narrowed their eyes at Harriet, and Georgina placed a steadying hand on Aunt Beanie's arm as she replied smoothly, "Thank you. It was very much a team effort. And we couldn't have done it without Sujin, our coach, and the support of Akemans antique centre and auction house and the Waterwheel Cafe."

"Of course," acknowledged Harriet.

Zach whispered to Dotty, "We must make Georgina our spokesperson. I love how she included our sponsorship in her response."

Dotty shook her head and gave a wry smile as Harriet continued, "We'd like to hold the prize-giving in five minutes if that's OK with you all."

"Is Gifford handing out the prizes?" Tani asked.

Harriet nodded.

"Then I must put my face on." By which Dotty believed she was referring to her make-up.

"And me," said Mel, glancing once again at Zach.

The two of them entered the changing rooms, with Olivia and Bryonie. Dotty heard their high-pitched laughter as the rest of the team followed them.

Aunt Beanie approached Dotty, Keya, and Zach and said, "I think I'll speak to Ned. He looked rather bemused by the revelations about Pip."

"Where is he?" Dotty asked. "I saw him walk off earlier."

"Don't turn round," advised Aunt Beanie, looking over Dotty's shoulder. "He's standing by the perimeter rail, staring out at the cricket field. But he keeps glancing at Pip, a morose expression on his face."

"Oh, I do hope this doesn't affect their relationship," Dotty said, her voice full of concern. She'd feel so guilty if it did.

"That's why I want to talk to him and try and include him in the team's celebrations."

"He was the one who encouraged Pip to take Dotty's place," Zach remembered. "And he was loving the match."

Aunt Beanie turned to Zach and said, "Actually, it might be better if you speak to him. Man to man. And try to persuade him to join us for the prize-giving. That way, he might feel part of the team and less confused about the situation."

"I'll do that," Zach agreed. He squeezed Dotty's arm and walked away.

As Dotty watched him, Keya said, "That was a good idea."

"I do have them," Aunt Beanie said imperiously and then stalked away to the changing rooms. At the entrance to the pavilion, she turned and called, "Are you two coming? We need to look our best for the prize-giving."

Dotty and Keya grinned at each other before moving to join her.

CHAPTER FIFTEEN

DOTTY

Despite the revelations about Pip— or Philippa, as those in the cricketing world seemed to know her— the prize-giving for the Three Counties Cup was a joyful affair.

Dotty joined Georgina and Aunt Beanie, standing to one side of the team. Next to her, Keya kept wobbling on the bench which she was standing on with Clara and Marion.

Mel and Tani had pushed themselves onto the front row, joined by Bryonie, Olivia, and Pip. Zivah stood on the far side of the bench, next to Zach, with Sujin in front of them.

They all beamed as they were announced as the winners of the ladies' cricket tournament. Dotty was surprised when her name was read out, and then thought Zach must have had something to do with it, as Akemans and Keya's cafe were also mentioned.

"Well done, ladies!" exclaimed Gifford Rivers, striding forward and positioning himself in front of Pip.

Tani shuffled to one side, so it was round her neck that Gifford placed the first gold medal.

"Hi, I'm Tani," she told him.

"Nice to meet you," Gifford responded automatically, as he reached for another medal from the basket Harriet was holding. But his attention was on Pip as he leaned down and placed the bright red ribbon around her neck.

"Is he going to kiss her?" Keya asked. If she'd meant it as an aside to Dotty, she spoke too loudly, as the whole team seemed to hear her, and Gifford pulled away hastily.

Dotty's gaze shifted to Ned, whom Zach had persuaded to join them on the field for the prize-giving. He was standing stiffly next to Aadi and baby Kaami, who were with Zivah and Keya's parents. Gilly Wimsey, Olivia's mum, was next to them, with a tall boy and girl who Dotty thought were Georgina's children. They were all smiling and clapping, and Ned joined in, though stiffly, as Gifford handed out the rest of the medals.

"And now, the presentation of the Three Counties Cup," Gifford announced.

Sujin stepped forward, pulling Zivah by the arm.

Zivah had said that Marion, who had acted as their captain that day, should receive the trophy. But she had refused, adamant that Zivah was the star of the team and of the day's match, and that she should enjoy the moment.

The crowd applauded, and photographers snapped pictures. Dotty kept a proud smile on her face as she looked around.

Nearby, Cliff, the groundsman, stopped pushing a heavy-looking metal roller and leaned against it, watching the prize-giving ceremony.

Hadn't he known Pip's real name earlier? He must have recognised her.

She saw Adrian Cartwright, Ashcombe Manor's deputy head, on the other side of the presentation party, and he did not look happy. Perhaps he'd placed a bet on the other team to win. His arms were crossed, and his feet were wide apart. And the look on his face was… thunderous.

CHAPTER SIXTEEN

DOTTY

"Good shot," Zach shouted, holding up one of the scorecards they'd all been given, with a six printed on one side and a four on the other.

He and the others seated in the temporary metal VIP stand waved the cards above their heads as music blared from the speakers. It was certainly a livelier atmosphere for the afternoon men's county cricket match than it had been during the ladies' game that morning.

Everyone settled for the next ball.

Dotty had a good view from near the top of the stand, not only of the play but also of the members' pavilion beside it. The area closest to them consisted of a cream stretch tent, the edges of which were secured by strong metal cables close to the ground on the sides and back, leaving the front open for viewing.

Behind the tent, the public area stretched out, with food and drink trucks serving refreshments to those not currently watching the cricket.

"This is fun," Zach said. "It's different from the ladies' match. More energetic and fast-flowing. But Sujin said that's because it's a short-format game."

"And the players are professionals," Dotty added. "It's clear most of the spectators are supporting the home side, Gloucestershire."

"Six!" cried the commentator as the ball sailed over the boundary rail and into a crowd of people seated on metal fold-up chairs.

"This is actually quite dangerous," Dotty remarked. "I hope the batsman doesn't hit a ball at us. I'd never catch it."

"Don't worry, I'll protect you," Zach said, sipping half a pint of Somerset cider from a plastic glass.

Dotty raised her eyebrows at him.

Instead of returning her attention to the game, she glanced around.

Their passes had allowed them to enter the VIP pavilion, where they'd been provided with lunch and drinks. Tani and Mel had dived into the wine, encouraged by Aunt Beanie. Since Dotty didn't see them in the stand, she presumed they were still in the refreshments area.

Close by, the two sisters, Georgina and Gilly, were sitting with their children, all of whom were enjoying ice creams.

"Poor Keya," Dotty said out loud. "Having to join Aadi in the sponsors' tent."

"She'll be loving it," replied Zach. "All those people congratulating her on her winning performance. It's Sujin I feel sorry for, but I suggested he sneak out as soon as he can and join us up here."

Another ball soared not only over the perimeter rail but also the seating area, landing dangerously close to the ice cream van, where families were queuing.

"The trouble is, this is a smaller ground," Sujin said, squeezing past two people at the end of the row above as he made his way to join them. "It's a school cricket field, and these players are used to much larger county grounds." He sat down behind them, leaning forward.

"Do people ever get injured?" asked Zach.

"Occasionally," Sujin admitted, "but I think they soon get over it as they're well looked after, and I suspect they receive tickets or swag from the club."

They watched the batters knock the ball around for another five minutes, until a particularly wild swing sent it towards the members' pavilion. It landed somewhere in the shadows at the back of the cream stretch tent.

"I hope that didn't knock the tea out of an elderly lady's hand," Zach said.

"Or her husband's whisky," added Sujin.

They chuckled.

"Help!" cried a scared voice.

Dotty, Zach, and Sujin stopped laughing and exchanged concerned looks.

"Maybe it did hit someone," Zach said, drawing his eyebrows together.

"What should we do?" asked Dotty.

"Nothing," Sujin replied. "There are plenty of trained medical professionals here. Look, there's one with a red bib running into the pavilion now."

Someone threw the ball back onto the pitch, and play continued, but Dotty kept glancing down at the members' tent.

She was surprised when, a few minutes later, a uniformed policeman wearing a high-visibility vest approached the group still huddled towards the rear of the pavilion.

"Oh dear, this could be serious," she muttered, but her words were drowned out by the crowd as the batter struck a four. The ball raced across the mown grass and over the painted white boundary marker.

Sujin's phone pinged.

"Oh no, that's a work message," he groaned, removing his phone from his pocket. With a note of surprise, he added, "It's Lynn," by which Dotty knew he was referring to Inspector Lynn Lockwood from Cirencester Police Station.

"She wants me to look at a case. At the cricket festival?" His voice rose a notch as Dotty looked down at the members' pavilion and saw Lynn standing there, speaking into her phone. She was clasping her young daughter Emily's hand.

"I was right," Dotty said with a note of regret. "The ball that landed in the members tent did do some serious damage. Lynn's there right now."

"And I need to join her," Sujin responded, standing up and inching back along his row. The people seated there muttered their displeasure.

"We should see if we can help," Dotty said, also standing up.

"Now, I don't think we should interfere," Zach warned.

Dotty looked down at him and said, "Well, at least I—we—could offer to look after Emily while Lynn works."

"Good idea. But this doesn't mean you can get involved in..." His voice trailed off before he added, "Anything."

The metal steps clattered as Dotty, Zach, and Sujin hastily descended them. When a uniformed security guard at the entrance to the members pavilion stepped forward, Sujin raised his official credentials and stated firmly, "Police".

Dotty and Zach quickly followed him. Dotty bowed her head, so she didn't have to speak, or lie to the security guard.

As they approached Lynn, who was still talking on her phone, a breathless Keya joined them.

"I know I wanted to get out of the sponsors' tent, but a body is a bit extreme."

Dotty stopped dead, and Zach side-stepped around her before also halting.

Keya ran into Sujin, who'd come to a standstill. "Sorry," she apologised, grabbing his arm. "But didn't Lynn tell you?"

"No, she only asked for my help." He looked pointedly at Dotty and Zach, and Zach responded with a shrug.

"We'd better see who it is. Probably one of the older members who suffered a heart attack when the ball landed in his cup of tea," Keya said, echoing the comments Zach and Sujin had made earlier.

They all approached Lynn and waited for her to finish her call.

"That was headquarters," Lynn said in a business-like tone, pocketing her phone. "They're sending a 'team', but we're to secure the scene and start the initial inquiries. But before we do, I need to warn you..." She looked at them all, including Dotty and Zach, who stood to one side. "...that you know the victim."

"We do?" Keya questioned.

Dotty thought of Harriet, the cricket official, in her smart black blazer.

Lynn nodded. "I'm afraid this will put rather a damper on your winning celebrations. Congratulations, by the way," she said to Keya.

"You were watching?" Keya asked, raising her eyebrows.

"The second half. I took Emily for a horse-riding lesson first thing this morning."

"Pony," corrected Emily, who Dotty remembered was only eight, or perhaps nine by now. "Today I rode Cassie. She's a lovely grey pony. Which means she's actually white."

Dotty noticed Lynn fidgeting awkwardly, so she said, "Why don't you tell me all about Cassie while your mum starts work?"

"And can I have an ice cream? Mummy promised, but then she got the call about the dead person."

"I feel like an ice cream," Zach said. "Chocolate. No, strawberry. Or maybe both." He grinned down at Emily, who giggled. Then he added, "Why don't Emily and I buy ice creams, and we'll meet you back near the pavilion entrance?"

Dotty smiled gratefully at him. She realised that she wouldn't be able to settle until she knew who'd died.

"You better put these on if you're joining us," Keya said, handing Dotty a pair of plastic booties. "And a hair net."

Suitably attired and putting aside any thoughts of how ridiculous she felt—it was a small price to pay for being included in the initial investigation—Dotty walked towards the back of the tent with Lynn, Keya, and Sujin.

The small group of people clustered there parted as Lynn and Keya stepped forward.

Keya gasped. "Oh no! It's Pip."

CHAPTER SEVENTEEN

KEYA

Keya stared down at the body of her cricketing teammate, Pip Lawton, or Philippa Lawson, as people in the cricketing world were calling her.

She was standing at the back of the members' pavilion, in a strange tent she had initially thought looked like an oversized bug, with curves and segments that reminded her of an insect's body. From where she was standing now, at the back, it stretched nearly down to the grass, and the area where Pip lay was in shadow. The people gathered around didn't help.

Behind her, she heard her friend Dotty—who shouldn't really be on the scene but whose observations were often invaluable—say, "Warren, Constable Sparrow, I wasn't expecting to see you here."

"They needed extra bodies, and I volunteered," he replied. "It meant I was able to watch Sergeant Varma, sorry, Keya's match earlier."

Keya smiled, despite the gravity of the situation. The young officer still seemed unsure how to address her. Until the end of the previous year, she'd been his superior at Cirencester Police Station. Now she was working with the force in her new role as a crime scene manager.

"This one's yours, if you feel up to it," Sujin said, joining her. "It won't be easy to process with all the people who've been here, both before and after the body was discovered."

Keya marvelled at how Sujin was able to switch into professional mode despite someone they knew—she'd go so far as to say, a friend—lying before them.

"A tragic accident?" Keya suggested, staring at the blood seeping from a wound on the side of the victim's head.

"I suspect so, but you know we must examine the evidence and not jump to conclusions. Dr Peter is on his way to give us an initial examination and pronounce Pip dead."

Keya hadn't seen Dr Peter with Gilly or Olivia, but perhaps he was on duty at the cricket festival. She was glad he would be attending the scene. Eccentric though he could be, he was also practical and knowledgeable.

Turning to Keya, Sujin said, "I presume Lynn's searching for Ned so she can break the tragic news."

Keya drew her lips together and nodded glumly. "I think so." She stepped away from the body and joined Dotty, who was standing by herself.

"Poor Pip," Dotty said sadly. "After returning to cricket with a fabulous win, she's killed by a cricket ball. If that isn't ironic…" Dotty looked dejectedly at Keya.

"Sujin says we mustn't jump to conclusions," Keya muttered.

"What? You mean she wasn't killed by a blow from that wayward cricket ball? The shot was hard enough to…"

"I'm not saying that. Only that we have to wait for the doctor to examine her."

"Someone talking about me?" asked a jolly voice.

They turned to watch Dr Peter approach. He believed physical exercise and fresh air were the cure for many ailments and set a good example by acting on his own words. Today, he must have been cycling, as he was dressed in black Lycra cycling shorts and a bright yellow top. His sandy hair glistened with sweat.

"Thank you for coming," said Sujin, stepping forward and speaking before Keya had a chance to. "The body is over here."

"Dad!"

Keya's eyes widened as Olivia ran into the tent.

Warren moved with surprising speed, stepping in front of her and blocking her path. "Sorry, miss, you can't go any further."

"Why does he always have to be working?" Olivia complained.

Dotty and Keya moved back to join Warren and Olivia as Dr Peter and Sujin moved towards the body.

The man at the entrance must have given up trying to regulate who did and didn't enter the members' pavilion, as Gilly, Georgina, and the rest of their children strolled in.

"Olivia," Gilly called. "Leave your father be. I'm sure he won't be long, and then he might join us for the rest of the match." She looked at Keya and Dotty, seeking confirmation, but there was a questioning expression on her face.

She must have registered their despondent looks because her demeanour changed. "Oh dear. A heart attack?" she asked.

Neither Dotty nor Keya replied.

"Let's watch the rest of the match. You can see Uncle Peter later," suggested Georgina as she ushered her daughter and son away.

Gilly's son, Thomas, was wearing a high-vis vest. Keya remembered that he wanted to join the police force, and as a member of the police cadets, he might be helping out today. "Olivia," Thomas called, "leave Dad be."

But Olivia had sidestepped Warren, who was answering a message or call, and Keya watched in alarm as she jogged towards Sujin and her father.

She stopped short and cried out in alarm, "Is that Pip?"

"Olivia!" Gilly called insistently.

Dotty approached Olivia and gently turned her away from the scene on the ground. "There's nothing you can do for her," she said softly.

"But… is she… is she…" Olivia repeated, unable to finish her sentence.

"Yes, I'm afraid so."

"Let Dad and the police find out what happened," Gilly said in a motherly voice, placing her arm around her daughter's shoulder. She looked at Dotty, her face full of concern.

Dotty mouthed, "Pip is dead."

"But we were all going to celebrate our win," Olivia cried. "How can we do that now? And what about next year?"

"Next year is a lifetime away, especially for someone your age. Who knows where we'll be or what we'll be doing," Gilly said, gently leading Olivia away.

As Dotty joined her, Keya said, "Give it five minutes and the whole team, if not the entire ground, will have found out what's happened. So, I'd better get to work. Are you OK here?"

"Yes, if you don't mind me watching."

"There's nothing new in that," Keya said, pulling on a pair of blue forensic gloves. "You've seen the police at work enough times before," she added with a wry smile, before calling across to Warren and asking, "Do you have any spare evidence bags?"

"I'll get some," he replied.

Keya took a deep breath and cleared her mind. She needed to treat this like any other crime scene, just as her training at the beginning of the year had taught her.

Turning back to Warren, she called, "And we need to secure the scene."

CHAPTER EIGHTEEN

DOTTY

Dotty stood in the odd-looking tent next to the main members' pavilion, watching the activity at the back.

Sujin and Dr Peter squatted beside poor Pip's body. They were taking their time with the examination, and Dotty hadn't heard Dr Peter officially pronounce Pip as dead. Was there a chance that the ball had just knocked her out, and she was still alive?

Keya still appeared to be treating the situation as a death, photographing the area with her phone. She took shots of several tables scattered with the remnants of sandwiches and cakes, half-drunk pints of beer, glasses of water, and other soft drinks. Would all of it need to be collected as evidence?

One of the tables and several chairs had been moved next to another, perhaps when people first rushed to help Pip, or simply to stand, staring morbidly at her body, much as she was doing now.

There had to be something useful she could do.

"Can you give Keya these evidence bags?" Warren asked, holding out a collection of plastic and brown paper bags of various sizes. "And I might need some help with the tape in a minute."

Dotty had no idea where Warren had acquired a roll of blue and white plastic tape from until he said, "Actually, Thomas can help me. He's already been running errands. Cadet Wimsey," Warren called.

Warren and Thomas fastened the police tape behind Dotty, and she took several steps forward, saying to Keya, "I have the evidence bags if you need them."

"Scene secure," Warren called. "What do you want us to do next?"

Keya took several close-up shots of one of the tables and its contents before turning and walking towards the tape, which Warren and Thomas had strung between two tent posts.

"It really depends on the type of crime we have and how thorough an investigation we need to carry out, but we do need to examine this area."

"Like CSI?" asked Thomas, his eyes wide with excitement.

"Exactly like that. So why don't you start with the sector just inside the cordon?" Keya suggested. "You'll need to wear booties over your shoes and gloves on your hands. Anything you find should be photographed in situ. You can use your phone for that. Then place it in one of the evidence bags Dotty is holding."

As Keya spoke, several members of their cricket team appeared, hanging back respectfully as Keya continued to instruct Thomas.

"You also need to mark where you found the evidence, if possible. But that won't be easy here. Maybe just write on the bag something like 'near the police tape', or 'one metre from the tape on the right'. If we suspected murder and had all our equipment, I would use flags to mark the evidence, or at least any major pieces we found. But we'll just have to do our best here."

The group standing behind Thomas had grown, and Dotty thought she saw all of the Coln Akeman Larks apart from Georgina Carey. Zach and Emily were standing to one side, eating ice creams.

"OK?" Keya asked, and Thomas nodded as he took the pair of booties Warren held out.

"What about us? How can we help?" Aunt Beanie called out in a serious voice.

"I'm not sure you can. Really," Keya replied, regretfully.

"It was an accident though, wasn't it?" Mel asked. "Someone said Pip was hit by a particularly long and hard cricket ball."

"That's what we believe, but nothing can ever be presumed at this stage," Keya explained.

"Look, Mummy!" Emily called. "Zach bought me an ice cream. And I told him all about Cassie and riding this morning."

"That's good," Lynn said. "What flavour is that?"

"Passion fruit. Zach said try something new. It's nice. A bit sweet."

Lynn smiled gratefully at Zach, then at everyone else standing around, and said, "You shouldn't really be here, but at least you're behind the police cordon. Thank you, to whoever put that up."

Warren and Thomas's cheeks both coloured.

Lynn approached Keya and asked, "What have Sujin and the doctor told you?"

"Nothing yet," replied Keya.

Lynn pulled a pair of booties out of her pocket and slipped them on. Then she ducked under the police tape and walked towards the back of the tent.

Keya followed her, and so did Dotty, although she kept her distance.

She heard Lynn ask, "She is dead?"

"Oh, most definitely," Dr Peter replied. "And she has a nasty dent on the side of her head."

"Consistent with being struck by a cricket ball?"

"Well, yes, but..."

"But?" Lynn repeated sharply.

Dr Peter looked at Sujin, who stood up and took a step back from the body. He turned to Lynn and said, "A cricket ball is round."

"I am aware of that," Lynn said drily.

Sujin ignored her tone and continued, "But the wound on her head, which likely includes a fracture to her skull, is squarer and larger than we would expect from the impact of a ball."

Dr Peter pointed at the body and said, "There is bruising and a laceration along the wound, with a small amount of blood. But there's also a darker area of bruising, most likely from the impact of the ball."

Lynn was silent. She stared down at Pip's prostrate form and said slowly, "You're not telling me this might be something other than an accident, are you? That she didn't die after being struck on the side of the head by a cricket ball?"

"She probably did," Dr Peter said, as he stood up.

"But you're not a hundred percent convinced?"

Dr Peter tapped his hand against his leg before replying, "Let's just say I still have questions that need answering."

Lynn sighed and turned to Keya. "Which means we have to treat this as a suspicious death and process the scene accordingly. Are you OK doing that?"

"Yes, although… my kit?"

"I'll grab our bags from my car," offered Sujin. "I threw your crime scene bag in with your kit bag this morning. I have no idea why, except they were sitting next to each other, and you never know when you might need it…" His words trailed off as he bowed his head and looked down at one of his former cricket players.

"I'd like to get ahead of this before the murder squad arrives," Lynn said. "But there are a lot of people to speak to."

"Perhaps we can help," suggested Dotty hesitantly.

"We?" enquired Lynn.

"The cricket team. Nearly everyone is here. We could speak to people in the members pavilion and ask for their details so the police can contact them later. I think I still see most of those who were gathered round the body earlier. But they might leave if a group of uniformed police officers arrives."

"So might I," muttered Lynn. Then she nodded and said, "That's actually a great suggestion. I think the members are more likely to speak to you lot as women and the winning team this morning. Let's see what we can sort out."

Sujin and Dr Peter remained with the body, and Keya moved away to speak to Thomas, as Lynn and Dotty ducked under the crime scene tape and gestured for Warren to join them.

Then Lynn addressed the Coln Akeman Larks. "We need to find out who was here when the accident happened and what they saw. There are lots of people in the pavilion, and it'll be impossible for Warren and me to speak to them all. So, Dotty suggested you could help us. You don't have to ask them those exact questions, but it would be useful to gather the names and contact details of potential witnesses, so we can reach out to them later."

"I'm happy to question them," Aunt Beanie volunteered.

"Good, but do it gently. Most of those I saw earlier were not in the first flush of life. Pip's death will have been a shock."

"Older people are more used to death than younger ones. They'll be fine," Aunt Beanie countered. "But I need something to write on and with."

"Warren?" asked Lynn.

Dotty saw a collection of police gear beside one of the tables.

Warren found enough pads, clipboards, paper, and pens for most of the team members. Bryonie and Olivia teamed up, and Clara joined Marion.

"Be civil and polite," Marion told Mel and Tani.

"We will," they replied defensively.

Dotty decided to walk along the back of the tent to reach members at the far end, near the other entrance to the pavilion, and stop them as they were leaving.

Most people were happy to speak to her when she told them she was working with the police and asked if they had seen anything connected with the earlier accident and the death of a cricket player.

People expressed their regret or sorrow, and a few enquired if the deceased really was Philippa Lawson.

Dotty replied politely but evasively to most of their questions.

One man said something that Dotty found interesting.

"I felt, rather than saw, the ball enter the tent, and I didn't see it actually strike anyone. A woman rushed after it and pulled away some chairs to find it. That was when she screamed."

"Thank you, that's helpful," said Dotty. "Could I take your name and address, in case the police need to follow up on what you saw?"

"I'm not sure I can add much, but of course," and Dotty wrote down his contact details. She was just thanking him when she heard a man calling out in a self-important voice.

"Ladies and gentlemen. I am Detective Sergeant Woodhouse of the Gloucestershire Murder Squad."

At the mention of murder, people began talking, and there were several exclamations.

"Which means," declared Sergeant Woodhouse, "that I need you all to remain where you are…"

Dotty missed the rest of his words, as she was swept through the entrance she'd been standing beside by a surge of people, all of whom appeared to have no wish to remain and speak to DS Woodhouse and his team.

Outside, she stopped behind another tent, next to a sign which read 'Sponsors'. She was soon joined by her teammates.

"That was fun," remarked Clara. "Like real police work."

"It was real police work," Marion replied. "And Inspector Lynn was right. I bet we found out far more than DS Woodhouse will. I've never seen some of the older members move so quickly when he told them they had to stay and speak with his team."

"There was something odd, though," Mel said, raising her voice slightly.

"What?" asked Aunt Beanie.

"Nobody I spoke to remembered seeing the ball actually hit Pip. What about the rest of you?"

Dotty looked round the group as they all shook their heads.

Aunt Beanie voiced what Dotty suspected they were all thinking. "Something doesn't feel right about Pip's death."

Nobody said anything as they drew their eyebrows together, pursed their lips, or tilted their heads in concern.

Dotty decided to share what she had overheard earlier. "And Dr Peter found some inconsistencies with the wound. It was larger and the wrong shape for a cricket ball."

Then, she remembered her recent conversation just before the murder squad had announced their arrival. "And someone I spoke to said the ball landed behind some chairs. Is it possible that Pip was there too?"

Aunt Beanie narrowed her eyes. "Standing, sitting, or… on the ground?"

Olivia's young voice rang out shrilly, "What if Pip was already dead?"

CHAPTER NINETEEN

KEYA

Keya used her official camera to photograph the area in front of where Pip's body still lay in the members' tent until Sujin said, "We're ready if you want to take pictures of the body in situ." He sounded calm and professional.

That was how she wanted to be. She took a deep breath and steadied herself before approaching Pip's body at the rear of the tent.

"I'll state the cause of death as blunt force trauma and describe the injuries, but I'll leave exactly how she attained them to you," Dr Peter said as he and Sujin stepped away from the body.

"And the time of death?"

"On the certificate, it will be the time I first examined her."

"And in reality?" Sujin pressed.

"Shortly before I arrived, but I can't tell you when exactly. The body temperature was perhaps a little cooler than expected, but not noticeably so, and there was no sign of rigor mortis."

"So death occurred within the last hour?" reasoned Sujin.

"Certainly, and it's likely to have been more recently."

"Thank you, Doctor," Sujin said as he and Dr Peter walked towards the front of the tent.

Keya took photographs of the body. She did think of it as a body now. The face was pale with a grey tinge, and the essence of the woman she had known was gone. Her voice, and her hesitant smile. None of it remained.

She leaned in closer to take shots of the wound. As she was doing this, she heard voices behind her, and a self-important man said, "You must be the local officer who called this in. I'm Detective Sergeant Woodhouse. I'll be taking charge."

"I thought you might, Sergeant," Lynn replied, her tone measured. "I'm Inspector Lockwood." Keya knew Lynn wasn't one for asserting her rank, but she also didn't tolerate rudeness. Still, she had negotiated an arrangement with the murder squad which still allowed her to investigate low-profile deaths, and Keya knew she wanted to keep it that way.

"And we have some of your crew processing the scene," DS Woodhouse continued, a note of derision in his voice.

Keya continued her work but smiled when she heard Sujin say, "Keya Varma is the official Crime Scene Manager, and I will be assisting her as the Regional Forensics Operations Coordinator. Any access your team wants to the scene will be through one of us."

Sujin rarely stated his official title or gave such direct instructions. He must have really taken a dislike to the murder squad DS. Perhaps they had history from previous cases?

"That may be so, but I want to see the victim."

"Of course," Sujin replied. "Here are some booties and a hairnet."

"I'm not putting THAT on," DS Woodhouse retorted dismissively.

"Then you can't see the body."

Keya stood up and turned round.

How did Sujin manage to remain so composed? His posture was relaxed, but it was clear from his position inside the cordon that the DS could only enter on his authority.

"Oh, very well," muttered DS Woodhouse as he pulled on the white hairnet. Behind him, other members of his team smiled or sniggered.

Keya rolled her shoulders and walked towards the group standing next to the crime scene tape. DS Woodhouse was exactly as she expected, although, as it was a Sunday, he wasn't wearing the sharp suit she was sure he wore to the office. Instead, he was dressed in a pair of light-coloured chinos and a short-sleeved, pale buttoned-down shirt. He looked like a former rugby player who liked his beer, and his belly was just starting to overhang his waistband.

But what really put her off was that he didn't have the manners to take off his reflective aviator sunglasses when speaking to Lynn and Sujin. He'd finally taken them off. Perhaps when he had realised how ridiculous they looked with his hairnet.

"Let's get on with it," he demanded.

He was a bully, Keya surmised as she ducked under the crime scene tape. And someone used to getting his own way by sheer intimidation. She smiled wryly, wondering just how he would fare working with Inspector Lynn. But then her smile froze. Lynn would most likely be taken off the case, and she'd be left working with the arrogant and probably heavy-handed detective sergeant.

She groaned as she removed her latex gloves.

"What's up?" Lynn asked brightly, a hint of mischief in her voice.

"I've just realised that you can hand this case over, but I'll have to work with the delightful DS Woodhouse," Keya replied, peeling off her forensic booties.

When she was done, Lynn led her towards the pavilion entrance. Lowering her voice, she said, "I don't think we should give up just yet. There's one person I'd like to speak to. Ned, Pip's partner. I've been looking for him, but I haven't seen him since the prize-giving earlier."

"I have," Mel said, behind them.

Keya turned to see the members of the Coln Akeman Larks standing just outside the members' pavilion. She and Lynn walked out to join them.

"I think we did rather well interviewing potential witnesses," Dotty said.

"Better than this lot," Aunt Beanie said, nodding towards the murder squad. Most of them were standing around, doing nothing.

"I'm not sure anyone has stayed to speak to them," Clara added. "Not after they heard the pompous policeman."

"What did you find out?" asked Lynn.

The team members summarised their conversations and, at the end, Olivia said, "We were wondering..." Her voice trailed off.

"Yes?" Lynn asked, intrigued.

"If Pip was dead before the cricket ball hit her."

Lynn's eyes narrowed as she leaned forward, clearly interested by the comment.

Olivia looked at Dotty, who said, "Not one person actually saw Pip being hit. In fact, nobody mentioned seeing Pip at all and, more than that, a man I interviewed said the woman who went to retrieve the ball had to remove chairs at the back of the tent to get to it."

"There weren't any chairs when we arrived," Keya said.

"Because they'd probably been moved already," Lynn considered.

"And then there's the wound," Keya raised.

"Yes," Dotty agreed.

Lynn recalled, "Which Dr Peter questioned, as it was larger and squarer in shape than he'd have expected from being struck by a ball." Her brow wrinkled as she stood straighter, gazing towards the cricket pitch and then back at the rear of the tent.

"It was a freak accident, being hit by a ball. And how hard would such a blow have been, after the distance the ball had travelled?"

"Very," Dotty replied. "I was getting anxious a ball might come our way, even though Zach said he'd make sure it didn't hit me."

"That would have been a tough catch," Aunt Beanie commented. "Sore on the hands, but worse if he'd missed it."

"So you're both saying that a ball hit by a cricketer at this distance could have killed Pip?"

"I believe so," Aunt Beanie agreed, her tone thoughtful.

"Particularly if she wasn't paying attention to the match and didn't know it was coming in her direction," Dotty added.

"Inspector," called DS Woodhouse, in a mocking tone.

Keya felt Lynn tense and then sigh. She joined her as they both returned to the area in front of the crime scene tape.

"I don't know why you called us out," began DS Woodhouse, as if he were telling off a wayward student. "It's pretty clear what happened here. The victim was standing at the back of the tent and didn't see the cricket ball – which was hit over the boundary – until it struck her. The impact was so severe that it fractured her skull and killed her. I'm sure the post-mortem will confirm death from blunt force trauma."

"I don't doubt it will," replied Lynn.

"Then why am I here?" demanded the DS, as he put on his aviator sunglasses.

"Does that mean you don't want the case?" asked Lynn, in an innocent voice.

"Of course not. Why would we? And you can have this ridiculous thing back." He dropped something on the floor.

Keya bent to retrieve the object and realised it was the hairnet. She smiled as she straightened up and saw DS Woodhouse stalk away, followed by his 'team'. They pushed rudely through the Coln Akeman Larks as they left.

"I'm pleased to see the back of them," Lynn said, sounding relieved. "Now we can start a proper and thorough investigation into Pip's death."

CHAPTER TWENTY

DOTTY

Lynn thanked the Coln Akeman Larks for their help and told them her team would now be running the investigation from Cirencester Police Station.

"But we want to do more," insisted Aunt Beanie.

"Yes" and "We do" muttered other members of the team.

"I know, and I can understand that. You've become a tightly knit team." Lynn paused, considering them. "I tell you what. Give us half an hour to finish processing the scene and arrange for Pip's body to be taken away. Then we can all meet to go through the case, and you can add any thoughts you have. At this stage, because there are several inconsistencies, I'm not dismissing Olivia's suggestion that Pip was dead before the ball hit her."

Lynn's voice became serious as she said, "Which means she either died of natural causes, or…"

"She was murdered," said Olivia, her voice tinged with excitement.

"But who'd want to harm her?" Tani questioned. "I know she was a big shot cricket star in her former life, but that was years ago."

"And I don't think the Evesham Eagles took out their disappointment over losing the match on her," Clara added.

There were a few weak smiles.

"But not everyone greeted her with a huge hug like Gifford did," declared Aunt Beanie. "And just why did she disappear, and feel the need to change her name?"

These were questions Dotty had been asking herself.

She saw Georgina and Gilly, along with Georgina's teenage children, approaching. Zach and Emily were with them.

Lynn nodded at the group of women. "Those are good points. So, while Keya and I focus on the death scene, why don't you lot, if you're willing, go round the ground and talk to people about Pip? Find out more about her life when she was playing cricket. Who were the people was she close to? And, of course, what happened that caused her to completely withdraw from the cricket scene?"

The Coln Akeman Larks exchanged excited glances.

"And Dotty, you know Ned, Pip's partner, don't you?"

"Not very well, but Zach spoke to him earlier and persuaded him to join us on the pitch for the prize-giving."

"It would be helpful if you two could find him but ..."

Realising her mother was looking at her, Emily rushed forward and exclaimed, "Look what Zach let me do."

Zach stepped forward and apologised. "I hope you don't mind."

Emily's face was painted like a unicorn, complete with a horn on her forehead, lots of pink, and plenty of glitter.

"You look beautiful," said Lynn, squatting down in front of her daughter. "But we'll need to wash it off before bedtime."

"Ohhh," Emily responded, clearly disappointed.

Lynn straightened up, looking thoughtful.

"Would you like Emily to come with us?" Gilly asked from the side of the group. "You don't mind, do you, Tilly? And James, we can find somewhere for you to sit to watch the cricket."

"You can use this tent," Lynn suggested.

Although most of the members had scattered when DS Woodhouse and his team had arrived, they were slowly trickling back into the pavilion. But there was still plenty of space.

"I'd like to help with the investigation," Georgina offered.

"I heard you helped solve a mystery while you were away in the Azores. Anything you can find out about Pip turning her back on the cricketing community would be useful." Lynn looked around the Coln Akeman Larks and asked, "Any questions?"

Marion, as usual, was the voice of reason. "What should we tell people happened to Pip?"

"Good point," Lynn acknowledged. "Tell them it looks as though she was hit by a cricket ball. You can even use what happened to start the conversations if you like. But remember, you are doing this voluntarily and unofficially. On no account say I've asked you to make inquiries. It could jeopardise my position and the case. I'm putting my trust in you because you're likely to find out more than that bunch who just left would, and because I think you genuinely care about what happened to Pip."

"We do," several members of the team chorused.

As they dispersed, Gilly approached Lynn and Emily. She asked Emily, "Would you like to come with me and Tilly?"

"Are you watching more cricket?" Emily asked uncertainly.

"Yes, but is there something else you'd like to do?"

"I'm bored with cricket. Can I watch TV?" Emily looked up at her mother.

"I don't have your tablet," Lynn replied regretfully.

"I have my phone," Tilly called. "And it has games on it."

"Yippee!" Emily called, and she skipped off to join Tilly.

"That's one problem solved, as long as you're okay looking after her," Lynn said, looking at Gilly.

"I might not be a cricket player or an amateur sleuth, but one thing I do know about is being a mother. And Emily is a wonderful, bright kid. I'm happy to help."

She walked towards the children and said, "Let's find somewhere to sit and then I'll sort out drinks. I need a cup of tea."

As Gilly followed the children, Warren called, "The ambulance is here."

"I'll go," Keya offered.

"I should too," Lynn said, before addressing Zach and Dotty. "But please can you two find Ned for me? I need to speak to him."

Dotty nodded, and she and Zach left the members' pavilion.

"What's going on?" Zach asked. "I think I picked up that there's some doubt about Pip being killed by a cricket ball. But if not that, how did she die?"

"I think Dr Peter was right when he stated the cause of death was blunt force trauma. But perhaps from something other than the cricket ball. Or maybe she was struck by the cricket ball and fell against something else."

"Like what?" Zach asked.

"I'm not sure. It seems as if the death scene, as Lynn is calling it, was disturbed when people tried to help, but even so, would one of the tables or chairs in the members' tent have done that much damage?"

Zach stopped and narrowed his eyes. "Are you suggesting what I think you are?"

"And what would that be?" asked Dotty innocently.

But Zach gave her a steely look, so she replied in a more balanced voice, "That I think there is more to this? Lynn isn't convinced the facts add up, and neither am I. So yes, I am considering the possibility that she was murdered."

CHAPTER TWENTY-ONE

DOTTY

As soon as Dotty had spoken the word murder, she began to doubt herself. But what was more likely? Pip being killed by a stray cricket ball, or someone from her past finding out that she was alive and, well, wanting to silence her?

Probably the former. But as she and Zach moved away from the members' pavilion, she recalled the morning and the excitement of the cricket match. The grounds of Ashcombe Manor School were much busier now, and the crowd watching the county match groaned or cheered along with the loud, jubilant music.

It was such a lovely day, with barely a cloud in the sky. A day to relax or celebrate, not to mourn the passing of a life.

Dotty judged Pip had been older than her, but probably not quite forty, so she'd still had so much to live for. And whatever had happened in her past, she'd seemed content with her life alongside Ned. But then, what did Dotty really know about the couple, or about Pip's life? She'd only met her a few weeks earlier.

"What are you thinking?" Zach asked, his voice soft.

"About Pip, and how tragic it is that her life was cut short."

"It happens to us all, eventually. Death," he said philosophically, as they paused to watch a group of boys and girls playing cricket behind the main public stand. They used yellow plastic wickets and a blue plastic bat, and shouted, arguing over whether the batter was out. Reluctantly, the boy handed the bat to a joyful friend, and the game continued.

As life would continue now, without Pip. It would affect her and the Coln Akeman Larks, sure, as their celebrations would be muted, but then they'd all move on. But for Ned, life would probably grind to a halt. The school holidays were still ahead of him. Had he and Pip planned a holiday, or maybe some time at the beach with their lovely little dog?

"We do need to find Ned," Dotty said.

A voice behind her remarked, "He's in the bar at the far end of the pitch."

"Thanks, Mel," said Zach, as his admirer joined them.

Dotty finally took note of what Mel was wearing, or more precisely, what she wasn't wearing. She was dressed in a tight, figure-hugging tube top and an extremely short denim skirt.

"I'll show you," Mel said, linking her arm through Zach's and leading him away.

Dotty followed, relieved when Zach extracted his arm from Mel's. She reminded herself that Zach was an attractive man with independent means, and it was only natural for women to be attracted to him. Women like her, she thought, blushing.

"What do you want to say to Ned when we find him?" Zach asked, slowing down to wait for Dotty.

"Um," Dotty replied, trying not to get lost in his concerned hazel eyes.

"What if he doesn't know about Pip's death?" Zach asked.

"I'm sure he does," said Mel, hanging back and waiting for them to catch up. "The way he was downing shots at the bar."

"But that might have been because Pip had been recognised, rather than the fact she was dead. Either one would likely be life-changing," Dotty reasoned. "I wonder how much Pip had actually told him about herself."

"Let's find out," said Zach. "There he is."

They had walked around the back of the temporary stands and other tents to reach the far end of the grounds.

Food and drink stalls selling everything from pizza to BBQ or

Greek souvlaki were arranged around the perimeter of the area, and at the end, there was a busy outdoor bar. It took Dotty a while to spot Ned, but then she saw him, staring ahead, leaning against a high circular table.

"Are you going to buy me a drink?" Mel asked Zach with a flick of her eyelashes which were heavy with mascara.

"Sure, it is hot, and I can see you don't have room for your wallet," replied Zach, with a playful grin.

Mel smiled in delight at the observation, while Dotty felt herself scowl with disapproval.

"That's right," Mel said, leaning closer to Zach.

"How much do you need?"

"I thought you might join me, and we could sit together and admire…" She paused deliberately. "The view."

Dotty rolled her eyes at the insinuation, but she was relieved when Zach said, "I'm afraid Dotty and I need to speak to Ned. Another time, perhaps."

Mel pouted with disappointment, before smiling slyly. "I'll hold you to that."

She sloped off as Zach turned to Dotty and asked, "So, how do you want to play this?"

"Naturally and sincerely," Dotty replied. "And you should take the lead. I think he trusts you. And although Lynn has asked us to find him so she can conduct an interview, we mustn't forget he's a victim too. He looks devastated."

Ned was leaning against the table. His sandy hair was even more unkempt than usual, and his glasses were askew.

As they approached, Dotty heard him mumble and then sob. This was going to be a difficult conversation.

"Hey, Ned," Zach said gently. "I'm glad we found you... How are you holding up?"

Ned squinted as he looked up at them, his brow furrowed in confusion. "Zach, what are you doing here?" He sounded disorientated.

"We came to find you. We were worried, after what happened to Pip."

Ned slurred, "She's dead, you know? My Pip. Gone."

"We really are very sorry," Dotty added, her voice full of empathy. "She was a lovely person."

Ned smiled crookedly. "She was, wasn't she? The centre of my universe. I was such a lucky man, but now?"

He reached down for his nearly empty pint glass and groaned, "I can't go on without her," before gulping down the rest of his beer.

Dotty felt Ned's pain in her chest. How must it feel to lose someone you truly loved? She fleetingly thought of her late husband, Al, and then her father and his struggle against cancer. But her eyes were drawn to Zach. What would she do if she lost him?

The thought caught her unawares, and she gasped.

Zach looked at her, his eyebrows raised in a questioning gesture, but Ned nodded sympathetically. "You understand, don't you? The void. The hole in your life. The realisation that she'll never walk through the front door, her face red from a run or clutching a mud-covered Willow." He stared down at his empty glass.

Dotty stepped forward and placed a hand on his shoulder. "I do. I lost my husband a few years ago. He was in the military and was killed during an exercise. I never had the chance to say goodbye."

"Neither did I," muttered Ned morosely. "And my last words to her were fuelled by emotion and hurt because she hadn't felt she could confide in me. Tell me who she really was."

"It must have been hard for her to turn her back on the cricketing world. But then she found you. And you gave her life new meaning." Dotty had no idea if what she was saying was true, but she needed to rouse Ned from his melancholy.

"Do you think so?" Ned asked, a brighter gleam in his eyes.

"Oh, I'm sure," responded Zach. "But look, you're not doing yourself any favours sitting here and drowning your sorrows. I know it's hard, but we need to deal with the practicalities of the situation."

"No, I just need to stay here," protested Ned.

Zach pressed on. "I've come to offer my help, and Dotty's good with the police..."

"Police?" Ned questioned, raising his voice.

"The cause of death is uncertain, so they have to investigate, even though it looks as if Pip was struck by a cricket ball."

"A cricket ball?" Ned blinked in confusion.

"Yes, that's how the police think she died. A freak accident after a ball was hit over the boundary," Dotty said.

Ned stood up and then stumbled.

Dotty gave Zach a quick glance as he stepped forward and said, "You're all right. I've got you. But I think we should find somewhere quiet to sit down."

Zach supported Ned, and they all returned slowly to the members' pavilion. As they were walking, Dotty spotted an ambulance and murmured to Zach, "Slow down."

She was relieved to see it drive away from the members pavilion before Ned spotted it. A few minutes later, they arrived at the pavilion's entrance.

Lynn was speaking to Warren and several other uniformed officers, and Keya and Sujin were crouched down in the area where the body had been found. The investigative work was continuing.

Lynn acknowledged their arrival but continued addressing the junior officers.

"Here we are," Zach said as he lowered Ned onto a white, upright chair with a gold seat cover. He rolled his shoulders. It must have been hard work supporting Ned all the way from the bar, but at least he was here now.

Dotty smiled gratefully at Zach and said, "What we all need now is a cup of tea."

Zach added, "And a slice of cake."

CHAPTER TWENTY-TWO

DOTTY

Dotty carried a tray with three teacups and a plate of cakes, bakes, and biscuits. But when she returned to the table where she'd left Ned and Zach, she found Lynn had joined them.

"I'll fetch another cup," she said as she placed the tray on the table.

"Let me," Zach volunteered. "I need some water."

Lynn was sitting next to Ned and looked sympathetically at him as she said, "I'm sorry for your loss. But there are questions I need to ask, and it's better that we do that now, rather than let them drag on. Is that OK?"

Ned nodded slowly.

Dotty added sugar to one of the cups of tea and placed it in front of Ned. "This might help," she said softly.

Ned lifted the cup in a childlike way, sipping its contents without objection. Pleased, Dotty added a slice of lemon drizzle cake to a side plate and slid it across to him. He broke off a piece and nibbled at it.

Dotty and Lynn sipped their tea, and Zach returned with a pint of water and a large slice of chocolate cake.

A tinge of pink returned to Ned's face. When he looked up, his eyes focused first on Zach, then Dotty, and finally on Lynn.

"When was the last time you saw Pip?" Lynn asked, her tone considerate but practical.

"There was the celebration on the pitch," Ned replied, "but it all seemed so surreal. Why didn't Pip tell me she'd been a cricket player? What else about her life hadn't she told me? Even her name was different."

"You had no idea about her former life as Philippa Lawson?"

"None. We only met a few years ago. I knew she was sporty. She'd worked as a games assistant at a school I was at in the Midlands. I couldn't believe someone like her would choose an unathletic soul like me. I prefer to bury my head in a good book rather than play tennis, squash, or any other sport. But I do like to walk. And so did Pip. It was one of the reasons I took the job at Farmor's and we moved to Coln Akeman. We even got Willow so we had no excuse not to walk every day, rain or shine."

For the first time, a smile tugged at the corners of Ned's mouth.

Dotty was relieved he had some pleasant memories. They would help him through the next few difficult weeks.

"It sounds as if you had a lovely life together," Lynn said with understanding. "But if you don't mind, I'd like to move on to more recent events. To today."

Ned tilted his head before responding. "I think I understand it all now. Her reluctance to join the team. She kept making excuses for why she couldn't attend training or the two matches she played in. It wasn't like her. She was so tough, and I questioned her about it. She always shrugged it off, but I think the only reason she came today was for me and for the team. I told her she couldn't let everyone down. How would it look if our village team arrived at the finals one player short? I told her that, as the new members of the community, we had to keep the team together. Eventually, she agreed to come."

"And when you were with Pip this morning, how did she seem?"

"Quiet. Slow. And she insisted on wearing that ridiculous oversized baseball cap, pulled down so low it almost covered her eyes."

"And when you arrived here, did you see or speak to anyone?" pressed Lynn.

"I saw plenty of people, but Pip kept her head bowed and no, she didn't say anything to anyone."

"So it was a shock to you when you found out she was actually former England ladies' cricketer Philippa Lawson?"

"She played for England?"

"Yes, for two seasons. She was very good."

"I wish I'd seen her play," said Ned wistfully.

"You did today," Dotty reminded him. "And the Coln Akeman Larks wouldn't have won without her."

"But at what cost?" Ned said, and now there was anger in his voice. "Her life. Our life. It would never have been the same again."

"No," Dotty agreed calmly. "But a relationship is better without secrets. You would have moved on. And I'm sure your support would have been invaluable. You might even have helped her to lay to rest whatever demons she ran away from in the cricketing world."

"You think I could have done that? Me? But I have nothing to do with cricket. And I'm not famous. Or talented."

"I believe you have other strengths," Dotty replied. "What about being loyal, supportive, and trustworthy? I'm sure those are qualities she valued, especially if she'd been let down in her former life."

Ned looked down at his hands. After a long pause, he said, "I hadn't thought of that. No wonder she looked so hurt when I accused her of lying... of deceiving me."

"When was that?" Lynn asked.

Dotty sensed she'd found an opening to continue her line of questioning.

"It was after the prize-giving, once she'd changed back into her everyday clothes. I didn't stop to think about her, or what it must have been like to face her past, and the people she'd deliberately left behind. I only thought about myself, and what others might think."

He looked up at Lynn and admitted, "After all the glamour and excitement of the match, I thought she was going to leave me."

CHAPTER TWENTY-THREE

DOTTY

Dotty sat down next to Ned and placed a comforting arm round his shoulder as he sobbed.

"I think that's enough questions for the moment," said Lynn, who was sitting on his other side in the members' pavilion. "But I do need to continue the investigation, and I'm not sure it's appropriate for you to stay here."

She directed her words at Ned but turned her gaze to Dotty.

"Why don't we help you find somewhere quieter to sit?" Dotty suggested, picking up on Lynn's hint.

Ned didn't respond, but his shoulders shook as he continued to cry.

"Come on, Ned, let's leave the police to their work." Zach gently helped him to his feet.

Dotty stood as well. "There's a space at that table over there. And Gilly's nearby."

As Zach guided Ned to the table, Dotty went over to speak to Gilly.

Emily was engrossed in watching Tilly play on her phone, while James and Gilly focused on the ongoing cricket match.

"Hi," Gilly said, shielding her eyes as she looked up at Dotty.

"Can you do us a favour and keep an eye on Ned, Pip's partner? He's... um, broken down."

"Poor thing. I'm not surprised," Gilly replied with sympathy.

"But don't let him have anything alcoholic. He's already had more than is wise today."

"Tea and water," Gilly nodded in understanding. "And what about you?"

Dotty turned as several members of the Coln Akeman Larks entered the pavilion.

"Team briefing," she said, before returning to the table where Lynn was still sitting.

Aunt Beanie, Marion and Clara were already seated at the table, and they were soon joined by Georgina, Mel and Tani.

Dotty sat down as Olivia and Bryonie arrived with Zivah, who waved briefly at Keya who was still working on the crime scene, before taking a seat at an adjoining table. Zach was the last to arrive. He cast a quick glance back at Ned's slumped figure before standing behind Aunt Beanie.

Mel looked up, patted the chair beside her and said, "There's space next to me."

"Thanks," Zach said appreciatively, "but I think I'll stand."

"So will I," Lynn said, rising slowly to her feet. "Thank you everyone." She addressed the group. "We've found Ned, by the way, but not surprisingly he's rather distraught about what happened. We'll keep an eye on him, but I might need someone to take him home."

"We could do that," Aunt Beanie offered, even though Zach had driven her and Dotty.

"Yes, I'd be happy to drive him back to Coln Akeman," Zach said without a trace of irony.

"Thanks," Lynn said. "And did anyone come across anything useful?"

Several members of the team nodded, but Aunt Beanie was the first to speak.

"I did," she said. "I went in search of Harriet Wintle, the recently appointed member of the Gloucestershire County Cricket Board. She credits herself with starting the Three Counties Ladies' Cricket Cup and she's devastated by Pip's death, or at least that's what she said. I have a feeling she won't mind all the publicity."

"But did she know anything about Pip?" Lynn asked, steering Aunt Beanie in a meaningful direction.

"Yes. She filled in the gaps in my memory of Philippa Lawson, the once rising star in women's cricket. Philippa, or Pip, took up the game in her late teens and was soon playing for Warwickshire, one of the leading sides at the time. Within a year, she was on the England squad where she excelled as an all-rounder."

"That was quite a career progression," Lynn commented.

"And her young, innocent face and humble background made her the perfect poster girl. Photographs of her wedding in Antigua were splashed across the front and back of every newspaper at the time. The glamorous young cricket star and the older England player. They were quite the celebrity couple."

"Of course," Marion remarked. "I'd forgotten she married a fellow cricketer, Adrian someone wasn't it?"

"Yes," Aunt Beanie replied, looking smug. "Adrian Cartwright."

Dotty gasped, but Lynn tugged her ear and said, "Should that name mean something to me?"

Zach frowned. "You don't mean the deputy head of Ashcombe Manor School, do you? That Adrian Cartwright?"

"The very one," Aunt Beanie confirmed. She stopped and glanced round to make sure everyone was listening. "And," she added, lowering her voice slightly, "Harriet Wintle doesn't think they ever got divorced because Pip, or Philippa, whatever you want to call her, just disappeared."

"That's what I don't understand," said Lynn. "Why would a young cricket player with a shining career ahead of her suddenly stop playing and completely retreat from the sport?"

"Oh, it was quite a scandal, I can tell you."

Dotty smiled to herself.

Aunt Beanie was enjoying being the centre of attention, and the one with all the details. "The golden couple of cricket. Except their marriage was tarnished."

"That's right," Marion recalled. "There was talk. Today we'd call it domestic abuse and coercive control, but back then it was generally seen as a matter between husband and wife. Physical abuse would have been frowned upon, but psychological or emotional? Nobody really understood it. But it was clear something was wrong, as

Philippa's game declined and she was dropped from the England team."

"Until she sought help from a young player in the Warwickshire squad," Aunt Beanie continued with a mischievous smile.

Dotty was learning a lot about Pip and her past from the tag team of Aunt Beanie and Marion, who were each adding to the picture of her former life.

"I remember some scandal, but I can't recall the details," Marion admitted.

"Neither could I, until Harriet enlightened me, and it's quite a revelation." Aunt Beanie paused again.

"What is?" Lynn asked, clearly unruffled by Aunt Beanie's dramatic pause.

"The young player Pip sought help from. The one she was rumoured to have had an affair with. It was none other than Gifford Rivers."

CHAPTER TWENTY-FOUR

DOTTY

"At least Pip had good taste," Tani remarked. Several members of the Coln Akeman Larks nodded as they sat at two tables in the members pavilion, facing Inspector Lynn, who was leaning against the chair next to Dotty.

"I wouldn't mind having an affair with Gifford," Tani added.

"You're not married," Mel pointed out.

Tani shrugged.

In a lower, more private voice, Georgina said, "I'm less sure about Adrian Cartwright, but perhaps he's let himself go since leaving cricket and becoming a teacher."

"Which brings me back to the case," said Lynn, looking at Aunt Beanie. "You're saying that Pip, or Philippa, married an older cricket player and, by all accounts, it was an abusive marriage. So she sought refuge with a younger player, and both of those men are here today?"

"Yes," Aunt Beanie replied succinctly.

"That's two suspects," remarked Olivia.

Lynn pressed her lips together. She didn't look entirely happy with the news.

Dotty considered the information Aunt Beanie and Marion had provided and then she said, "I think I now understand the animosity between Adrian and Gifford. At our auction a couple of weeks ago, Adrian was bidding for a bat, but then Gifford arrived and bid much higher than he needed to secure it. In fact, I think the bat is on display somewhere in the members' pavilion today."

"Buying a cricket bat is hardly a crime," Tani pointed out, clearly defending Gifford.

"No, but Gifford must be loaded," Mel said. "What fun to be able to buy things other people want just to put their noses out of joint."

"And I think that's what Gifford did," Dotty agreed. "And now I understand the comment Adrian made when he saw Harriet with Gifford this morning when we arrived."

"Oh yes," Zach recalled. "Wasn't it something about Gifford being one for the ladies?"

"He said Gifford was always a ladies' man," Dotty confirmed.

"'Was', as in, in the past," Lynn considered. "And I'm guessing he wasn't using a humorous tone."

"Definitely not," replied Zach. "I wondered at the time what history there was between the two of them, but I didn't know Adrian had been a serious cricketer."

"Oh, yes," Aunt Beanie responded, turning to look up at Zach. "He was one of England's top batsmen for several seasons, but when he met Pip, he was past his best. Some reporters wrote rather unkindly that he only married Pip to galvanise his own career and remain in the spotlight."

"Perhaps they were right," Georgina remarked dryly.

"But how does all of this help Pip? Do you think one of them deliberately killed her? But if so, how? And why?" asked Clara, frowning.

"Those are interesting questions," Marion agreed, before looking at Lynn.

"To be honest," Lynn answered, running her hand through her dark, shoulder length hair, "I don't know. All this information could mean everything or nothing. And as for how and why she was killed, I was hoping you might have some ideas."

"I think you should question Adrian," Dotty suggested. "No wonder he was looking annoyed at the prize-giving. His 'wife' was one of the star players."

"And Gifford," Lynn nodded, "if he's not involved with the county match. I think I heard him commentating earlier."

Zivah spoke for the first time. "If you want to know more about Pip and her past, it might be worth talking to that reporter."

"Clare Savage?" Zach asked.

"Yes, she seemed to know about Pip and her previous relationships."

"And she knows the sporting and cricketing worlds. The parts the public see, and the parts they don't," Zach added.

"I'll add her to my list," Lynn acknowledged. "Anyone else?"

Dotty thought of all she'd seen and heard that day. Then she said, "Actually, there was someone who knew who Pip was before the rest of us."

"Oh?" Lynn said, and all eyes turned to Dotty.

"I heard the groundsman call her name, her real name, when she finished batting."

"If he knew who she was, maybe others did too," Aunt Beanie mused.

There was a brief silence as the group absorbed this information.

Dotty asked, "What did Pip say on the cricket field, after Clare and Gifford had recognised her?"

Marian replied, "She told us she was sorry for deceiving us, and then she revealed that she'd played cricket for England."

"Which I suppose explains a few things. And to think I played alongside a former international player." Zivah sounded thoughtful.

There was a brief silence as the group absorbed this information.

Zach said wearily, "I thought cricket was a game for gentlemen…"

There were several coughs and protests from members of the Coln Akeman Larks.

"But now I'm beginning to wonder if it's just another game of secrets, betrayal, and lies."

Zivah spoke again. "Talking of secrets and potential betrayals, and of the groundsman, Cliff, Olivia, Bryonie, and I had an interesting chat with him just now."

"He grew up in Antigua," Olivia said, her voice full of wonder.

"I didn't even know where that is," Bryonie confessed.

"It's in the Caribbean, and Cliff said the sea is crystal clear and there are coral reefs and wonderful sandy beaches. Can you imagine that?" Olivia said wistfully.

"Why would he want to leave that to work as a groundsman in dreary old England?" Mel asked, raising an eyebrow.

"Cliff wasn't always a groundsman," Zivah said in a compassionate tone. "As a rising star on the West Indian cricket circuit, he sought his fame and fortune over here, but it was much harder than he'd expected. He even asked me if I'd ever considered being a professional cricket player and if my ethnicity and lack of connections had put me off."

Olivia looked at her, awe in her voice. "Would you like to do that?"

Zivah chuckled. "A village cricket team, playing alongside my friends, is a far cry from the pressures of the professional game. And besides, I'm a bit old to start now, and I have family commitments."

"You're not that old," Georgina said. "None of us should let our age or the troubles life throws at us stop us from growing and seeking out our dreams."

"True," Zivah replied. "And that's what Cliff did. He reached for his dreams, but…" Her voice trailed off.

"Cliff blamed the old boys' network for not making it as a cricket player in the UK. But what does that mean?" Bryonie asked.

Aunt Beanie jumped in. "He's referring to an age-old, unofficial system where people, mostly men in the past, gain advantages through connections and friendships rather than through merit. It's always been informal, of course, but everyone knows it happens."

"Oh, is that why Cliff was so bitter? Especially about his boss, Adrian Cartwright? He said Adrian should have left cricket, but his celebrity marriage kept his career going."

His marriage to Pip, Dotty considered, which Cliff knew all about.

"It must have been hard for him," Zivah sympathised. "He admitted the competition was strong, and he struggled to pay the bills."

"Is that why he became a groundsman?" Tani asked.

"I guess so," Zivah said, sounding sad.

"He doesn't like his boss, though," Olivia revealed.

"Yes, he really dropped him in it," added Bryonie, smiling conspiratorially.

"What they're both failing to tell you," Zivah said, looking at Lynn, "is that after the prize-giving, Cliff saw Adrian approach Pip. She tried to pull away, but he grabbed her arm. Cliff didn't think Adrian was congratulating her on her performance or the team's win. When I asked if he'd heard anything, he clammed up, but you might want to speak to him about it."

"I probably will," Lynn agreed, sounding weary. "But you've convinced me that the next person I need to find and interview is Pip's ex-husband. Adrian Cartwright."

CHAPTER TWENTY-FIVE

KEYA

"I'm not Philippa's ex. I'm still her husband. We didn't get a divorce." Adrian Cartwright rocked back on his heels as he regarded Lynn with a smug expression.

Keya was eager to tell Lynn what she'd found, but she slowed as she approached the members' bar, where Lynn was facing Adrian, Pip's former husband. Or perhaps not. If what she had just overheard Adrian say was true.

Leaning nonchalantly against the bar, he continued, "Philippa did a runner. Just vanished. So the divorce process was never initiated, never mind completed."

Keya approached steadily. Lynn glanced briefly at her before asking Adrian, "So what did you think had happened to your wife?"

"That she'd been ditched by that spineless opportunist the moment he realised his own career was at stake," Adrian said bitterly. "He left her to take the fall, exactly as I always suspected he would."

"Who is 'he'?"

"Who do you think, detective? Golden boy Gifford Rivers. Though his star wasn't shining quite so brightly back then, believe me."

"And why do you say that?"

"Because that's the truth. But do your job, detective. Ask him what happened rather than waste your time questioning me about my wife." He spat out the last words.

Changing tack, Lynn asked, "Would you say your marriage was a happy one?"

"Happy? Who has a happy marriage? But it was exciting. We were both playing for England, and it was exhilarating and busy. We had practices, matches, and tours. Often we only caught up on the phone."

"And when you did spend time together?"

"What is your question, Inspector?"

Lynn paused briefly, appearing to choose her words carefully. "Mr Cartwright, marriages end for many reasons. I know that from personal experience, but some causes are more serious than others. Your wife chose to disappear completely rather than simply ask for a divorce. Did anything happen between you? Something she might have been too afraid to speak out about?"

Adrian stared back at her, his eyes hardening in his ruddy face. "Exactly what are you insinuating, Inspector?"

"I'm not implying anything, Mr Cartwright. I'm simply asking whether Pip had a reason to feel unsafe or perhaps threatened. Something that might explain why she chose to vanish without a trace."

Adrian folded his arms tightly across his chest. "I resent that question, Inspector. Our relationship was passionate, intense even, but I would never have harmed Philippa."

"I can understand your resentment," Lynn said calmly, holding his gaze. "But you can appreciate why I have to ask. Your wife left her life behind entirely, which is unusual, especially for someone with a promising career like hers."

Adrian looked down at the glass sitting on the bar, his jaw tightening. "Philippa did what she wanted. As she always had. Maybe she simply got bored. Maybe being a cricketing star wasn't enough for her anymore. Maybe you should ask Gifford."

"I will be speaking to Mr Rivers," Lynn replied in a level tone. "But if there is something you haven't mentioned, perhaps an argument between you, or some other incident, it would be better to hear it directly from you rather than from others."

Adrian picked up the glass.

Although the liquid was clear and Keya spotted a slice of lemon floating in it, she doubted it was water or any other soft drink. Probably gin with a splash of tonic.

Adrian slowly sipped his drink, visibly composing himself. Then he replied, his voice tight. "Inspector, I don't know what you are implying, but I have nothing further to add. Our marriage ended years ago. Philippa made her choice clear when she left, and until today I hadn't set eyes on her. That's all there is to it."

"So you haven't seen her since she disappeared?" Lynn asked smoothly.

Adrian shook his head sharply. "No. Not once."

"Until today," Lynn added quietly, watching him closely.

Adrian's cheeks flushed, anger flaring briefly across his face. "Of course I saw her today. I could hardly miss her winning performance, although why she let that amateur have all the glory, I have no idea."

Keya clenched her fists. She presumed Adrian was referring to Zivah.

Adrian curled his lip briefly in contempt before continuing, "Seeing her here was a shock. I had no idea she'd resurfaced or was even alive, for that matter. You can imagine how surprised I was."

"Did you speak to her?" Lynn pressed.

Adrian hesitated, his voice growing tighter. "Barely. We exchanged a few words, but with all the fuss around the cricket, I didn't consider it the right place for a proper conversation."

Lynn raised an eyebrow, but her tone remained steady and neutral. "A witness saw you with Pip. They described your exchange as heated. Certainly not friendly."

Adrian's eyes narrowed defensively. "People see what they want to see. I was understandably upset that she'd reappeared after years without a word. Perhaps I raised my voice, perhaps it looked tense, but that doesn't mean anything. And it certainly doesn't mean I harmed her. Besides, I wasn't the one who hit that cricket ball. Great shot, though. One I would've been proud of back in my day."

He paused briefly, eyeing her coldly. "And now, if there's nothing else, Inspector, I have a cricket match to watch."

He picked up his drink, took a hearty slug, and turned towards the cricket field. Without looking back at Lynn and Keya, he stated, "And I wasn't the only one who spoke to Philippa. You might ask Harriet Wintle why she was in such a rush to leave the members' pavilion before this afternoon's match."

Then, walking steadily, he moved away from them.

As he did, Lynn breathed out noisily.

"He's a difficult one to crack," Keya said sympathetically.

"I don't know what I expected," Lynn admitted. "Remorse, perhaps? Regret for how he treated Pip during their marriage?"

Keya shook her head gently. "Men like Adrian don't think they've done anything wrong. He's probably convinced himself Pip is to blame for everything that's gone wrong in his life. Was he actually a good cricketer?"

"I'm told he was one of England's top batsmen." Lynn nodded thoughtfully, her gaze still following Adrian's retreating figure. "But his career fell apart after Pip left. He's had years for that resentment to fester. Seeing her today would've stirred it all up again." She shrugged. "But he's right. He didn't strike the cricket ball that supposedly hit Pip."

"Supposedly?" questioned Keya, the excitement of her discovery building inside her again.

"No witness saw it hit Pip."

"That's interesting," Keya said, clenching her fists in anticipation.

Lynn turned and gave her a keen look. "Why is it?"

"Because I don't think the ball killed her either."

"You don't? What have you discovered?"

"An old wooden cricket bat with what looks like blood on it."

Lynn's eyes widened as she asked, "The murder weapon?"

CHAPTER TWENTY-SIX

DOTTY

Dotty was sitting with the Coln Akeman Larks, who were half-watching the second innings of the men's county match while continuing to discuss Pip's death.

Music and applause rang out around the cricket ground.

"That's Gloucestershire's first wicket," said Zivah, standing up. "And, if there's nothing more I can do to help here, I should get back to Aadi. Kaami will have woken from his nap, and Aadi has his clients to entertain."

She paused, watching Keya and Lynn approach.

Both wore serious expressions, but when Keya glanced at Dotty, she grinned briefly.

Something had happened, but Dotty had no idea what.

"If that's all, sis," Zivah said to Keya, "I'll go back to the hospitality tent. But if you need any more help or if find anything out, you will call me?"

Keya nodded, and Zivah smiled briefly and sadly at her teammates before leaving the members' pavilion.

Lynn looked thoughtful as she slowly studied the Coln Akeman Larks. Her gaze rested on Aunt Beanie, who stared enquiringly back.

"Is there something you'd like me to do?" asked Aunt Beanie.

"I'm not sure, and it is rather irregular," admitted Lynn.

"Even better. You want me to do some snooping?"

"Actually, I need to find out why Harriet Wintle was seen rushing away from the members' tent just before the county match. I'm not sure it has anything to do with our case, but..." Her voice trailed off.

"You want me to check." Aunt Beanie sat a little taller.

"You seemed to have developed a rapport with her, and I need to see what Keya has discovered..."

Everyone turned to look at Keya, who dropped her gaze to the floor and shuffled her feet. She wasn't giving anything away.

"But it would be best if someone went with you," Lynn said, glancing round the group.

Several hands shot up in the air.

Dotty looked at her former teammates and smiled. The Larks really were keen to discover exactly what had happened to Pip.

"Dotty," Lynn said, making her jump.

She turned to look up at Lynn.

"Can you go with Bernadette? You've witnessed police interviews before, and I need someone level-headed to make sure everything is covered."

"Are you saying I lack restraint?" Aunt Beanie asked, rising to her feet and arching an eyebrow.

Lynn sighed. "I'm saying this is all unorthodox and unofficial, and two people are better than one."

She looked wearily at Aunt Beanie, who grinned and patted her arm. "Of course. I'm happy to help in any way I can. Come on, Dotty."

Dotty stood up, shrugged, and hurried after Aunt Beanie. "Where will we find Harriet?"

"Let's start in the officials' stand, which is the upper section of the pavilion where we changed this morning."

Dotty didn't ask how Aunt Beanie knew this as she jogged to keep up with the long, purposeful stride of her older companion.

"What do you think happened to Pip?" she asked.

"At first, I thought, like everyone else, that she was hit by that stray cricket ball. It does happen. People get injured, but rarely fatally."

"And now?" Dotty pressed.

"Like you, Olivia, and the rest of the team, I'm not so sure. But I do feel sorry for Pip. To have to give up her career because of the actions of others." She pursed her lips and shook her head. "Men," she muttered under her breath.

Aunt Beanie rapped sharply against a door marked 'Officials'.

"Yes?" said a young woman with a polite smile when she opened it several minutes later.

"Please can you tell Harriet that Bernadette Devereaux is here, and the police have a few more questions for her?"

The young woman's eyes widened in surprise, and she blurted, "Yes, of course. Right away," before slamming the green, wooden-slatted door in their faces.

Aunt Beanie raised an eyebrow and waited.

A few minutes later, the door opened again, and the smartly dressed Harriet stepped out. "Shall we move around to the lawn?" she suggested.

They followed Harriet, who paused briefly to speak to a muscular man guarding the entrance to a fenced-off grassy area. The first three rows of seats were occupied by people dressed similarly to Harriet, but she led them to a section at the back where several chairs had been removed from a row and rearranged into a circle.

"Let's sit here. We can still see what's happening on the field without being overheard. Janelle said the police wanted to speak to me, so why are you here?"

"I know it's a little unorthodox," began Aunt Beanie, "but our friend, Inspector Lynn Lockwood, is trying to manage on her own after a group of arrogant officers arrived from Gloucester Headquarters, decided the crime wasn't worth their effort, and left."

"And Lynn has to complete the paperwork, which is why she needs to report what happened," Dotty added. "The trouble is, Ned is in such a state we're struggling to work out who was the last person to see Pip before she died."

"She was very much alive when I left her in the members' tent," Harriet responded seriously.

"And when was that?" Dotty pressed.

"Just before this match started. I was with her and Ned, and then I heard the announcement that the players were about to come out onto the field, so I excused myself and hurried over here. The first ball was about to be bowled as I took my seat upstairs on the officials' balcony."

"How did Pip and Ned get into the members' tent?" asked Aunt Beanie, frowning.

"Oh, I invited them," Harriet replied. "Many of our members are... how shall I put this? Getting on in years. So they remembered Philippa from her playing days and were delighted to see her again. One of them even took the 'Invincibles' bat out of its frame and handed it to her so he could take a picture of her with his wife, and also pretending to play a shot. Philippa was very sporting and played along, as she always did. I'm not sure Ned was quite as comfortable with all the attention, though."

"I think finding out that Pip had a past life, and that she was once famous, has unsettled him. Add her death to that, and it's no wonder he's had too much to drink and can't function properly."

"Poor man," Harriet said gently. "But I'm not sure I can be any more help. As I mentioned, I heard the announcement that the players were about to take to the pitch, and I left the members' pavilion. That was the last time I saw Philippa. She was holding the cricket bat as if it were part of her, standing next to Ned and talking to her admirers. I hope she enjoyed those final moments."

"So do I," murmured Aunt Beanie.

"And how did Pip seem when she was with you?" Dotty enquired.

"Rather bewildered, really. But that wasn't a surprise. After all, she was being plunged back into a world she left some fifteen years ago. But it was so good to see her." Harriet smiled sadly.

"And did you notice anything suspicious?" asked Aunt Beanie.

"Like what?" Harriet sounded troubled. "I thought Philippa was killed by a cricket ball. But these questions... was she...?"

Dotty interrupted quickly. "As we said, it's just for the police paperwork." She shot Aunt Beanie a warning look. "Unless there's anything else you think is relevant, we'll leave you to enjoy the rest of the match."

"All I would say is that I'm pleased she found someone as dependable as Ned. She hasn't been lucky with the men in her life. Nor with her friends, for that matter. For Clare Savage to betray her like she did. It was unforgivable."

Dotty jumped at the sudden outburst of noise around the ground.

Harriet sprang to her feet. "Yes! That was the wicket we needed to take. Please excuse me."

Dotty watched Harriet hurry out of the fenced area and back to the players' and officials' pavilion.

"I don't think Harriet had anything to do with Pip's death," Aunt Beanie said in a disappointed tone. "And I'm sure we could find the members she was speaking to. Besides, what motive would she have? It would only be good publicity for her and Gloucestershire County Cricket to have rediscovered Philippa Lawson playing in their Ladies' Cup."

"I think you're right. But did you catch what she said at the end about Clare Savage? That was interesting."

"Interesting enough to find out more?" asked Aunt Beanie with a knowing look.

Dotty shrugged her shoulders, but she knew she was deceiving herself when she replied, "Only if we bump into her on the way back to the members' pavilion."

CHAPTER TWENTY-SEVEN

KEYA

"I can't be certain this bat was used to hit Pip on the head, but we can't rule it out," Keya said, squatting down beside an old wooden cricket bat. It was darker in colour — seasoned, Keya thought — than the bats she and her fellow Larks played with. Several strands of string wrapped around the handle were fraying, and along both the front and back, she could just make out faded writing.

"Is that darker area at the end blood?" Lynn asked as she squatted down.

After a brief examination, Keya had returned the bat to the place she'd discovered it, in the shadows at the corner of the tent, where the stretched canvas nearly touched the tufts of short grass.

"No, the colour is mostly due to the bat's age, but it does make it harder to spot any drops of blood. I've already taken photographs and made a sketch of it in situ, so when you're ready, we can pick it up and examine it more closely in the light."

Lynn stood up and looked around.

Just inside the tent, several of the white members' chairs had been placed haphazardly. Lynn tapped the top of one and said, "These would have made an effective screen, keeping the bat out of sight from any casual observers."

"I agree," Keya replied. "But what was the point of hiding it here?"

Lynn tilted her head, considering the question before she responded. "Neither the bat nor the body were hidden in a way that suggests the perpetrator, if there is one, didn't want them to be found. More that they were concealed for as long as possible before being discovered."

Keya nodded. "If that ball hadn't been hit in this direction, and if the lady who retrieved it hadn't moved the chairs, it's unlikely Pip's body would have been discovered today."

"That's my thinking. It could have lain here all day, possibly until tomorrow, when the clearing up started. And the same goes for the bat."

"But why didn't our culprit take the bat with them? It would hardly look out of place at a cricket match."

"It might if they weren't a player, and none of our current suspects are. Plus, even I can tell that this is a vintage bat and not the type used today." Lynn looked up and said, "I wonder what Sujin thinks?"

Keya straightened up and smiled weakly as Sujin approached.

"The body has arrived at the mortuary," he said. "I've spoken to the pathologist and asked him to examine our victim's head under proper lighting and to give us his initial thoughts. He won't be conducting a full examination until at least tomorrow afternoon. He has several heat-related deaths from the weekend to deal with first. That is, unless he also has doubts that the death was caused by a stray cricket ball."

Sujin finished his update and looked from Lynn to Keya, then down at the ground. "Which he might well have," he muttered, squatting down beside the bat.

Keya presumed he was still referring to the pathologist.

"Was this the bat sold recently at Akeman's auction? The one signed by Don Bradman and his Invincibles?"

"I'm not sure," Keya replied. "I only examined it briefly before telling Lynn about it. But it's old, and covered in faded writing."

"I've seen enough in its current position," Lynn said. "You can move it now and see if there's anything else it can tell us. And whether there really is any blood."

Sujin raised an eyebrow at Keya.

"I'm just speculating," she said, pulling on a second pair of blue latex gloves. "But I thought there were darker, glossier patches. We need to examine it in brighter light."

Carefully, she picked up the bat and carried it across to a table beside which she and Sujin had left their crime scene kit bags earlier.

Her teammates had moved away. Marion and Clara were watching the match while Georgina was sitting next to Gilly. Keya caught her glance at the adjacent table where Ned was still slumped. Perhaps he'd fallen asleep.

Laughter erupted from Olivia, Bryonie, Tilly, and Emily, who were all huddled together.

Keya tilted the bat in her gloved hand until the flat surface caught the light. The writing, a collection of signatures, some accompanied by a line or two, stood out more clearly.

Her eyes worked their way down the bat to the darker end.

"Is that what you found earlier?" asked Sujin, who was now also wearing a pair of latex gloves. He pointed to a slightly raised, glossy patch. It was small and easy to miss among the bat's other markings.

"Is that it?" asked Lynn, sounding disappointed.

"Let's check," said Sujin, his tone businesslike. He turned to Keya. "Would you like to carry out the test, or shall I?"

"I'm holding the bat, so why don't you test it?" Keya responded.

"It could just be caked dirt or a scuff mark," Lynn considered.

"It's on the striking face of the bat, not the base, so it wouldn't be a scuff mark from the ground," Sujin replied, opening his bag to search inside.

He removed a swab in a sterile plastic packet and a box of Hemastix strips. The latter had a clinical use for testing blood in various liquids, but they were also a quick and generally reliable method for detecting blood at a crime scene.

Opening the plastic packet, he rolled the swab forwards and backwards over the patch Keya suspected might be blood. Then he pressed the swab against the end of a thin strip of paper with a yellow tip.

For a moment, nothing happened.

Then, as the chemical reacted, a vivid green stain spread up the strip.

Lynn's eyes narrowed. "What does that mean?"

"That blood is present," Keya replied with satisfaction.

"Technically, it means the reagent on the strip has reacted with haemoglobin. But effectively, yes, it confirms that spot is blood," Sujin explained. "What it can't tell us is how long it's been there or when it landed on the bat."

"And it will need to be tested in a lab, but…" Keya said excitedly, "it provides another explanation for how Pip died."

Sujin took the bat from her and turned it in his hands as he studied it. "And one that is more consistent with Dr Peters' examination of the wound. He questioned how a round ball could create a rectangular imprint."

He bent his head as he examined an area near the bottom of the bat. "And what's this? Can you pass me my tweezers? And we'll need a small evidence bag."

Keya had worked crime scenes with Sujin before and she knew where he kept things in his bag, which was far more organised than her own.

She found both items and handed Sujin the tweezers.

He used them to extract something caught in a splinter of wood.

She held up the evidence bag as he dropped in what looked like several short, light-coloured hairs. Hair that was very similar to Pip's.

"We might be able to match the DNA on those to our victim," Sujin said.

"Shall I prioritise them with the lab?" Keya asked.

Sujin nodded. "I would."

Keya placed the bag on the table and wrote her details, along with the time, date, and location of the discovery.

As she did so, she heard Lynn ask, "So where does this leave us?"

Sujin didn't answer, so Keya turned back to face them and said, "With an unexplained death that we need to treat as suspicious."

"Then I'll have to continue my interviews. Warren has taken Thomas to question people in the grounds. Dotty and Aunt Beanie …"

"Aunt Beanie?" Sujin interrupted, sounding sceptical.

"She used to work with the police in the Rural, Heritage and Wildlife Unit, until it was… disbanded," Keya explained.

"I didn't know that," Lynn admitted. "But I asked her to speak to Harriet Wintle again, as she seems to have an understanding with her.

I sent Dotty as well, to keep the discussion on track and find out more about our victim. And also why Harriet was seen rushing away from the members' pavilion."

"You don't think Harriet was involved, do you?" Sujin asked, sounding even more doubtful.

"At the moment, I have no idea. Up until several hours ago, our victim was living a quiet life in Coln Akeman. Then, suddenly, she was thrust back into the spotlight. Ever since, we've been uncovering aspects of her past that she—and others—might have preferred to remain there," Lynn explained.

"So if this is… I'm just going to say it as it is… murder," Keya stated, "then who are your suspects?"

"At the moment, those we know had a past relationship with our victim include her still-husband, Adrian Cartwright, and her former lover, Gifford Rivers. Other names linked to the investigation are Ned, her current partner, the groundsman, Cliff, the reporter, Clare Savage, and Harriet, who we've already spoken about. Although why any of them would have a motive to kill her, I've no idea."

"Then that's what we need to find out, I guess," Keya said. "Where will you start?"

CHAPTER TWENTY-EIGHT

DOTTY

Dotty paused to watch the new batsman stride onto the pitch as Aunt Beanie said, "The visitors have a healthy score, but Harriet was right. That last wicket for Gloucestershire might prove pivotal."

Dotty didn't enquire further about the match. She was thinking about the reporter, Clare Savage, as she asked, "Do you think there's a press room or area?"

"There's bound to be, likely somewhere around here. Still hoping to just 'bump into' Clare Savage?" Aunt Beanie raised an eyebrow.

"No, but I do think we need to talk to her. After all, Lynn has an entire case to run. She can't speak to everyone," Dotty reasoned in a serious tone.

"I like your logic," Aunt Beanie said with a grin.

They looked around, but there was no obvious press area.

Then Aunt Beanie gestured. "Over there. There's a 'PRESS' sign pointing to the back of the stone building next to the players' and officials' pavilion."

They followed a gravel path past a set of toilets and round the back of a two-storey building to a discreet black door set into an alcove. A printed 'PRESS' sign was stuck to it at an angle.

"I guess we try here," said Aunt Beanie, knocking unenthusiastically against the metal door. A hollow thud echoed dully. When nobody answered, she tried again, but there was still no response.

"I'm not surprised," Aunt Beanie remarked as they made their way back along the gravel path to the main area. "I wouldn't want to be holed up in there on a glorious day like this."

"And Glamorgan need to keep up the run rate if they're going to catch Gloucestershire," the commentator announced.

"That's Gifford, isn't it?" Dotty queried.

"And for the next over, I'll hand you back to Dominic," Gifford's voice came through a nearby tannoy, mounted on a metal post at the edge of the cricket field.

As Dotty and Aunt Beanie picked their way past the officials' lawn and the players' pavilion, she felt frustrated about not finding Clare.

She wanted to help Lynn, of course, but she also wanted to speak to Clare and find out whether she had been a friend of Pip's and, if so, why Harriet had hinted that she had betrayed her.

They approached the commentators' box just as someone inside called, "Another four!" There was a smattering of unenthusiastic applause amongst the spectators.

Aunt Beanie stopped suddenly, and Dotty glanced at her, also coming to a halt as the noise around them subsided.

Then she heard hushed voices. Glancing around, she was surprised to see Gifford, head bowed, speaking to Clare Savage. They were standing behind the commentary box. The very place Dotty and Aunt Beanie had been heading towards.

Clare said something Dotty didn't catch, then smiled smugly as Gifford shook his head. He looked bewildered as he glanced up and noticed Dotty and Aunt Beanie.

"No. Not at all. I don't know how you can think that, never mind ask me?" he said to Clare before striding quickly around the side of the commentary box.

Clare frowned as she watched him disappear, his form still visible through the back window of the commentary area.

"He made a hasty escape," commented Aunt Beanie as she

approached Clare. "Were you by any chance asking him about Philippa Lawson?"

"I might have been," Clare replied defensively, then suddenly smiled.

Dotty tensed, immediately wary of her.

"You were one of her teammates, weren't you? You have that... unique bowling style."

"If you mean an unorthodox way of taking wickets, then yes. I can hardly be a pace bowler at my age," Aunt Beanie retorted, but she couldn't hide a hint of pride.

Clare conceded the point and relaxed, and so did Dotty.

"You actually did surprisingly well. And if Philippa's death hadn't overshadowed the competition, I had a nice piece ready about village cricket and amateurs."

"I'm sure it would have been complimentary," Aunt Beanie responded in an ironic tone.

"Mostly," Clare conceded. "That Zivah Patel is a great player. She could be a professional."

"She's content playing at amateur level," Aunt Beanie replied with a warning note.

"Oh, well. Perhaps the piece will be printed at some stage, or published online. But tell me, how was Pip as a teammate? Did she take over and tell everyone what to do? You must have guessed she'd played at the top level."

"Actually, no," Dotty said, stepping forward. "It was a complete coincidence she played at all. It was only after I was injured and her little terrier ran after the ball that we discovered she could throw straight, never mind bat and bowl."

"Philippa has a dog?" Clare asked innocently.

"Yes, and we'll tell you its name after you've given us some information. About Pip." Aunt Beanie stood taller and folded her arms across her chest.

"So you want to know about Philippa do you? What did she tell you?" Clare stared back at Aunt Beanie, her eyes lively with curiosity.

"Nothing," Dotty began, but Aunt Beanie cut in.

"As I said, tit-for-tat. You tell us something, we tell you."

Dotty wasn't entirely sure this was how police interviews should be conducted, but then, this was hardly an official discussion.

"Very well." Clare smiled, and Dotty had the impression she respected Aunt Beanie. Perhaps even considered her a worthy opponent. "Ask me a question."

But this time, Dotty jumped in. "How did you betray Pip?"

"I..." Clare opened her mouth, then swiftly closed it again. She looked surprised, even shocked, by Dotty's question.

Dotty pressed. "You were friends, weren't you? Did she confide in you? And did you use that information to tarnish her name?"

"I'm not sure who you've been speaking to," Clare blustered.

"Someone important, who knows cricket and its setup very well," Aunt Beanie replied with an air of authority.

"Yes," Dotty added. "A reputable source said you let Pip down."

"She did that all by herself," Clare countered. "Sure, she may have spoken to me about the business, but she knew what was going on. That was clear. Besides, all my comments were speculation. I was very clear about that."

"But people still believe what they read," Aunt Beanie remarked. "And if you accused Pip of cheating, she was hardly in a position to protest. Not once it appeared in print."

"Is that what you think I did? Accused Philippa of cheating? At cricket? No. Although, perhaps you're right in a way. Deceitful, lying... and perhaps what she did would be considered cheating by some people. The public certainly weren't happy about it."

As Dotty wasn't sure exactly what Clare was talking about, she was slow to form another question.

Spotting the opportunity, Clare asked, "The name of Philippa's dog?"

"Willow," Dotty replied, unhappy to lose control of the discussion. Just what had Clare been referring to?

"Of course. Like the wood cricket bats are made from."

Dotty thought quickly. It was their turn again, and she needed another question. "Where were you between the cricket matches?" she asked, since Clare's potential involvement in Pip's death was what they were supposed to be investigating.

Clare shrugged. "Lots of places. Some of the time I was at the sponsors' tent with Gifford. I grabbed some lunch, and then I returned to the press area to write up my notes."

It would be hard to prove the latter, Dotty thought, but there should have been plenty of witnesses in the sponsors' tent. Gifford, for one.

"And did you speak to Pip?"

"Now, now. My turn. How long have you both known Pip?"

Aunt Beanie looked at Dotty and shrugged.

Dotty replied, "We don't live in the same village as her and Ned. But I think she moved there quite recently. Ned teaches at Farmor's School in Fairford."

Clare jotted down her response and was about to ask a follow-up question when Aunt Beanie asked, "Did you speak to Pip after the prize-giving?"

After a brief pause, Clare cleared her throat and replied resolutely, "No."

But Dotty wasn't sure she believed her.

"When was the last time ..." Dotty began, but Clare wagged a finger at her.

"No, no. My turn." Clare turned and looked directly at Dotty as she asked. "Did Philippa ever mention anyone from her past?"

This time Aunt Beanie answered, and copying Clare's style, she stated an emphatic, "No."

Clare sighed. "I can see we're at an impasse, and there are other people I need to speak to." She turned back to face Aunt Beanie and, with an amused smile, added, "But it was fun sparring with you." Then she strode away, glancing around as she went.

Dotty moved to stand beside Aunt Beanie. Watching Clare's retreating figure, she asked, "Did we give more away than we learned?"

"The name of Pip's dog and Ned's job. Not exactly world-shattering news. But we've established she knew Pip in her cricketing days and that she wrote an article about something to do with a business Pip was involved in. Whether she let Pip down as Harriet suggested, we don't know, but I wouldn't put it past her."

"And I'm sure she was lying about speaking to Pip after the prize-giving."

"Me too, and her alibi was rather vague. If there is anything malicious behind Pip's death, then Clare is definitely still a suspect."

"Although Pip probably had more of a reason to harm Clare than the other way round."

"There's more to find out about that one," Aunt Beanie said as Clare stopped to speak to someone. "It's just a matter of how we go about uncovering it."

CHAPTER TWENTY-NINE

DOTTY

Dotty and Aunt Beanie decided to return to the members' pavilion and update Lynn on their findings, but before they got far, Dotty spotted Lynn walking towards them.

She looked tired and far from happy to have a potential murder to investigate on her Sunday off.

She slowed when she saw them and, as she approached, she asked, "Have you found our murderer?"

Aunt Beanie and Dotty exchanged a brief, concerned glance before Dotty enquired, "Are you saying Pip definitely wasn't killed by that cricket ball?"

Lynn updated them on Keya and Sujin's findings with the cricket bat. "It's not conclusive," she added, "but all the circumstantial evidence is mounting up. So I definitely need to treat this case as a murder inquiry. And I'm afraid that means any interviews now need to be taken formally by myself or Warren."

"But we can still help," insisted Aunt Beanie. "Like finding witnesses who saw Clare Savage after the prize-giving. She said she was with Gifford in the hospitality tents and then in the press room, but the latter is isolated, and I doubt anyone was with her."

"You've spoken to Clare? And to Harriet?"

Dotty and Aunt Beanie gave Lynn a not-so-brief summary, with Aunt Beanie frequently adding her opinion on the conversations.

"Anyway," Dotty concluded, "I'm not sure Harriet had anything to do with Pip's death, but Clare? I'm certain there's more she wasn't telling us. And we need to find out about the past, and what she wrote that caused so much trouble."

Lynn nodded. "That's a job for the officers at the station. I'll get them to do some searching on the internet tomorrow."

"Of course," Aunt Beanie declared. "Clare mentioned publishing online. I wonder if her old article is still there."

"It's difficult to entirely delete anything once it's on the web, so probably," Lynn acknowledged.

"Then please excuse me." Aunt Beanie flashed a smile before turning on her heel and striding away.

"Where's she going?" Dotty questioned.

"She seemed taken with the idea of finding Clare's old article about Pip, but she can hardly do that from here, can she?" Lynn shrugged and, ignoring her previous question, asked Dotty, "Have you seen Gifford Rivers?"

"He's in the commentary box, but I don't think he's actually working at the moment. In fact, I think he hid there just to get away from Clare. They were having… not heated words, but rather an agitated discussion before Aunt Beanie and I arrived."

"Really?" Lynn considered this, looking brighter. "I like it when threads of an investigation start to interweave. And if our suspects are jumpy, they're more likely to let something slip. Let's find Gifford."

"I thought you said it had to be official now," raised Dotty.

"I said I or Warren needed to speak to the suspects. I said nothing about you being with me." Lynn looked happier now as she chuckled to herself and approached the door of the commentary box.

When Dotty reached it, Gifford was already walking calmly down the wooden steps.

There was nowhere in front of the box where they could speak without being overheard, so he led them away to a spot between the cricket field and the outdoor bar, where she and Zach had found Ned earlier.

"Mr Rivers," Lynn began.

"Please, call me Gifford. Everyone does."

Lynn hesitated, appearing uncomfortable with the informal start to her questioning, but she took a breath and started again.

"Gifford, it's clear from your reaction earlier that you were very fond of Philippa Lawson."

"Fond of her? I loved her. I always have."

Dotty couldn't help herself and blurted out, "So why did you let her down?"

Instead of giving her a reproachful look, Lynn nodded and followed up with, "Yes, please tell us about your relationship with Philippa and how it ended."

"Do you mind if I have a drink?"

Lynn didn't have the opportunity to protest, as Gifford was already striding towards the bar. When they caught up with him, he was ordering a Macallan, which Dotty knew was a single malt whisky.

"Ladies?" Gifford offered politely.

Dotty was thirsty. "Just a water, please."

Lynn didn't answer, so when the young woman behind the bar set a small plastic glass on the counter containing an amber-gold liquid and smiled widely at Gifford, he requested, "And two waters."

She placed two metal bottles beside the whisky along with two empty plastic glasses.

Gifford paid for the drinks and handed Lynn and Dotty each a white bottle with blue writing on it.

"Let's talk over here," he suggested, moving towards the back of the bar area. He sat down on a high stool, placing his drink on one of the tall, circular tables.

Dotty also took a seat, but Lynn remained standing.

"Mr Rivers. Gifford," Lynn began for the third time. "It would be really useful if you could tell us about your past history with Philippa and, as I believe you had a relationship with her, what caused that to end?"

"Is it necessary to rake that up? We've all moved on," he said, picking up his glass and staring into it. "To bring it back... well, it's rather painful."

"I'm sure it is, but as the lead investigator in a sudden fatality, I have protocol to follow."

In other words, Dotty thought, Lynn was using official language to cover up that this was probably a murder investigation.

"Oh, I see," Gifford said warily, although he clearly didn't.

"So, your past relationship with the deceased?"

Gifford took a slow sip of whisky, then sat back and raised his eyes to the clear blue sky.

"It was such a wonderful time. The best of my life. Of course, we kept our relationship quiet to start with, as I was worried about how Adrian would react. He had a nasty temper, especially after a few drinks. And although he was cruel—what you'd now call abusive—to Philippa, he never laid a hand on her. But I was worried he would if he found out about our affair."

He lowered his gaze, looking concerned.

"Eventually, when the rumours became too much for even the self-centred Adrian to ignore, I persuaded Philippa to leave him. She refused to move in with me, but at least she was away from him. We could both focus on preparing for the upcoming cricket season. And what a summer it was. Philippa played brilliantly at both county and national level, and I made it onto the England team as one of their top bowlers."

"Was Adrian still playing for England?" Dotty asked.

She presumed, from all the talk, that he had represented his country, but she wanted to be sure.

"He was hanging in there because they were short of experienced batters. And oh, did he resent me. I had to keep to the far end of the changing rooms, and our teammates had to pull him off me on more than one occasion. There's one thing Adrian values above all else."

"And what's that?" asked Lynn, playing along.

"His ego, image, and status in the cricketing world."

Which was three things, Dotty thought, but ultimately represented one trait. Adrian was a narcissist.

"So he resented Pip leaving him and having a relationship with you?" Lynn kept her expression neutral and professional.

"Resented? He hated it. I could see it eating away at him, and do you know what? I think it still does. That Philippa finally had the courage to turn her back and walk out on him. He could never accept it or admit he'd done anything wrong. From that moment on, any issue he had, he blamed it on Philippa. He was very vocal about the effect their break-up had on his game. Those in the know understood better, but to the general public, it made them question the innocent young player they'd taken to their hearts."

"Do you mean Pip? But I thought you two were rather a... golden couple." Or at least, Dotty remembered, that was what Aunt Beanie had called them.

Gifford smiled, as if reminiscing over a fond memory. "That's a great way of putting it. And we did have a fabulous time, attending fashionable parties and important events. We even went to the premiere of the final Harry Potter film in Leicester Square."

"So what went wrong?" asked Lynn, breaking the spell.

"I... um..." Gifford picked up his glass and drained the rest of his whisky.

Dotty prompted, "Was it anything to do with an article Clare Savage wrote?"

"You know about that?" For the first time, Gifford's eyes showed a hint of fear.

"We do. Not all the details yet, but they'll be easy enough to find," confirmed Lynn.

"It wasn't my fault Clare blamed Philippa. They were supposed to be friends, and I've no idea why she turned on her like that. But I had my career to think about too."

"So you betrayed Pip to save yourself," Lynn declared.

"It wasn't like that," Gifford protested, picking up his empty glass and staring at it. "Or perhaps... that's exactly how it was," he conceded.

"Which is why you've felt guilty and wretched about it ever since. Did you have the opportunity to apologise to Pip?"

"Not until today. She vanished soon after the article was published. The public really did turn on her and take my side." He had the good grace to blush.

"When she refused to answer my calls, I went round to her cottage, but it was empty. Her neighbour said a van had come a few days earlier, and the driver told her the contents of the cottage were going into storage as the occupant had gone abroad. And that was the last I saw of Philippa until today."

"You didn't try to contact her?" Dotty enquired.

Gifford shook his head miserably. "I knew if she wanted to disappear, I wouldn't find her."

"And then you saw her today," said Lynn. "How did that make you feel?"

CHAPTER THIRTY

DOTTY

"I was elated," Gifford replied, smiling broadly. "At first, I thought the player who walked onto the pitch to bat at the end of the innings was a doppelgänger. I think that's what you call them. And then when the American coach…"

Dotty smiled. Zach would be chuffed that Gifford had called him a coach.

"…told the commentary team the player's name was Pip Lawton, I just knew it had to be my Philippa, even though she played well within her capability."

He cocked his head and added, "You must have seen my greeting. I was so excited I completely lost myself in the moment."

Dotty remembered how Gifford had flung his arms round Pip, lifted her up, and spun her around.

"I just couldn't believe it."

"And you said you spoke to Pip? When was that?" Lynn asked.

"After her match, just before lunch. I was walking across to the hospitality tents to speak to some of the guests when I spotted Pip and Clare together. And I can tell you, I don't think that friendship was going to be rekindled."

Interesting, thought Dotty. Clare had been lying, just as she and Aunt Beanie had suspected.

She asked, "Did you happen to hear any of their conversation?"

"I wasn't trying to eavesdrop, but I could tell Philippa was furious. They certainly weren't making amends. She accused Clare of twisting the truth and making her the scapegoat, which is exactly what happened. And Clare didn't deny it. She just… stood her ground, like she had nothing to apologise for."

Dotty was intrigued, wanting to find out more about Clare's article and what she'd accused Pip of, but Lynn asked, "So you saw Pip and Clare together?"

"Yes, but as I approached, Clare looked at me with what I can only describe as indifference, although I'm sure I saw a flash of resentment. I'm not sure why she asked if I felt guilty and was just trying to make myself feel better. It was a strange comment."

Not strange at all, Dotty thought, if Clare was projecting her own feelings onto Gifford. Her remarks were actually quite telling.

"And that's when you spoke to Pip too?" Lynn prompted.

"Yes. Clare made another cutting remark before leaving us, but at least I had a moment to talk to Pip alone. Not for long, though, as she said she was looking for Ned and needed to explain a few things to him. Is it true he had no idea about her past? That she was a cricket star?"

"We believe so," replied Lynn.

Ned had told Dotty and Zach that he and Pip had only met a few years ago.

"Such a shame Philippa felt she still needed to hide her old life," Gifford murmured.

Dotty considered this aloud. "From what I knew of her, she wasn't one to dwell on the past. Whatever happened back then, I think she'd found a way to move forward and create a life she was content with."

Gifford nodded thoughtfully. "I think you're right. I hope she was able to move on and find happiness. She said she didn't blame me for what happened, that we were both young, and that others had manipulated us." He grinned. "And she admitted we did have fun."

Then he shook his head. "Maybe we could have done again. If only that freak accident hadn't happened."

Dotty glanced at Lynn, but her expression remained neutral.

"At least I left her on a positive note," Gifford continued. "Before I left to address the corporate guests, I told her I'd love to catch up with her and Ned."

He hesitated before adding, "But you might want to talk to Clare. She was hanging around, and I saw her approach Pip again after I left. I thought about going back, but I had the feeling the new 'Pip,' as she called herself, could handle Clare. I hope she did," he added philosophically.

"To be clear," said Lynn in her best police officer voice, "you left Pip at around…"

"Lunchtime," Gifford replied.

It was a vague response, but then, Dotty wouldn't be able to track the day by time either. Only by the action on the cricket field and the events surrounding Pip's death.

"And you didn't see her again?"

Gifford shook his head. "I'm sorry to say, I did not. And after that, I need another drink." He picked up his plastic glass and returned to the bar.

Dotty unscrewed the lid of her metal water bottle and took a sip. The water was cool and refreshing.

"Does what Gifford told us help?" she asked Lynn.

"It does, if he's been truthful about speaking to Pip, especially in respect of the timing, as it gives us another marker for her movements following the prize-giving. But I need to speak to Clare to corroborate it."

"And do you still view Gifford as a suspect?"

Lynn exhaled. "He really is the darling of the cricketing world, but was his pleasure at seeing Pip again and his hope of rekindling their friendship sincere, or just a front?"

"I think he's being genuine," Dotty reasoned.

"Unfortunately, so do I," Lynn agreed. "And what motive would he have to harm Pip? If anything, she'd be the one to hold a grudge against him, not the other way round."

"Unless he hasn't told us everything." Dotty frowned. "What if he did see Pip again in the members' pavilion, and this time their conversation turned heated? Maybe Pip was holding that old cricket bat and, in a moment of anger, Gifford grabbed it and swung it at her. He's certainly strong enough."

"I don't know how much force would be needed, but it's a plausible scenario." Lynn tapped her fingers against the table.

"But I just can't see them fighting like that," Dotty said slowly. "Not after what I've witnessed today."

"We still don't know everything," Lynn pointed out. "You assume Pip had made peace with her past betrayals, but what if she hadn't? What if she was the one who became angry, and Gifford was only trying to protect himself?"

"Would he really hit her with the bat?" Dotty questioned.

"Maybe. In a struggle." Lynn shrugged. "That's a question to raise with Keya and Sujin."

CHAPTER THIRTY-ONE

DOTTY

Lynn and Dotty watched as Gifford downed another fortifying whisky. He didn't return to their table but instead ambled slowly back towards the players' and officials' pavilion.

Dotty wondered whether, despite the alcohol, or perhaps because of it, reality was beginning to sink in, and he realised someone he'd once cared for deeply had died today. Or maybe he simply needed a break from the constant buzz of the cricket festival, to take a moment and process everything.

"I think we're making progress," Lynn mused as they wandered slowly back towards the members' pavilion.

"I still can't find any credible motive or reason why our current suspects would harm Pip," she continued, "but there's so much about her past we don't yet know. Perhaps the answer lies there. If we don't wrap the case up today, there'll be plenty of research for the junior members of my team to get started with on Monday."

Dotty nodded. She didn't have anything to add.

Inside the tent in the members' pavilion, Keya and Sujin were seated at the table they'd claimed as their own, speaking to someone on Sujin's phone.

But Dotty and Lynn were drawn to a cluster of activity at another table. Aunt Beanie was sitting beside Georgina, and Bryonie, Clara, and Olivia were with them. All of them had their phones out, but Dotty had the impression they weren't simply scrolling through social media.

When they were in earshot, Dotty heard Clara say, "This one doesn't mention Pip, but it is about Gloucestershire Cricket Club."

"And is there anything relevant in it?" Aunt Beanie enquired hopefully.

"Um," replied Clara as she scrolled through her phone. "It mentions selling information about the players, and who'll be in a team. I'm not sure why that matters." She scrolled again. "Oh, I get it now. The reporter, Alex Crawford, alleged that someone at the club was exchanging information for cash to the benefit of a group of bookmakers."

"I doubt that had anything to do with Pip," Georgina remarked.

"You're right, there's no mention of her, but, um…"

"What is it?" Aunt Beanie asked bluntly, as she regarded Clara.

"It mentions another player. A West Indian called Clifford Hamilton. Do you think that might be the groundsman here? He's called Cliff and we know he's from the West Indies."

"Only one way to find out," Lynn announced, making Clara yelp in surprise. "Is there anything else in the article I should know before I go and interview him?"

"More details about the bookmakers, and a demand for the authorities to make an example of the perpetrator for bringing cricket into disrepute."

"The final nail in the coffin, in case any reader had their doubts about the player's innocence. Guilty by public opinion," Aunt Beanie concluded, sounding resigned.

"Not if it was true. Someone has to speak out against improprieties. Otherwise, it's worse for the sport, which gets accused of covering up or failing to deal with its internal issues," Georgina commented.

The debate continued as Dotty followed Lynn out of the members' pavilion. Lynn hadn't invited her along, but then again, she hadn't told Dotty to stay behind either.

"That could be a motive," Lynn said as Dotty caught up with her.

Catching her breath, Dotty replied, "I presume the article Clara found was an old one, as the Clifford Hamilton it referred to was a player, not a groundsman."

"True, but if the allegations were from the past and never proven, yet Pip knew the truth, and Cliff was aware of that, then seeing her today would have come as a shock. He might have wanted to silence her. And who pays attention to a groundsman? Like a waiter, they're often overlooked as they move around at events like this."

Dotty followed the logic, although she wasn't entirely convinced.

"There he is, leaning against the perimeter rail," said Lynn, quickening her pace.

As they approached the edge of the cricket field, Cliff lifted his baseball cap, scratched his short white hair, and put his cap back on.

"Mr Hamilton," Lynn said formally. "I'm Inspector Lynn Lockwood, and I'm conducting enquiries into the death of Pip Lawton, previously known as Philippa Lawson."

Cliff leaned back, his shoulders and arms tensing.

"There's nothing to be afraid of. I just need to ask about your relationship with Pip. I take it you knew her when you were both players?" Lynn asked in a more relaxed tone.

"We weren't in the same club. She played for Warwickshire, but I saw her. Mostly when she supported her husband."

"Adrian Cartwright, who is now your boss."

"That's right. He might have his faults, but I'm indebted to him for finding me this position."

Indebted was an interesting choice of word. Dotty thought that grateful might have been more appropriate in the circumstances.

"So that's when you met Pip? When she was married to Mr Cartwright?"

"Yes, and everyone thought they were the perfect pair, but I knew differently. She confided in me, she did."

"Why do you think she did that?" Lynn enquired keeping her tone casual.

Cliff shrugged. "We were both different. On the edge of cricket. Her being a woman and me, well..." He shrugged again. "There was more than one occasion I found her crying. Adrian could be very cruel. I knew that, and although I didn't like it, I had to accept it."

"So you weren't surprised when Pip left Adrian for Gifford?" Dotty asked.

Lynn nodded in agreement and waited for Cliff's response.

"No. Actually, I was delighted for them both. They seemed to bring out the best in each other. Their careers took off…"

"But yours didn't?" guessed Dotty.

"No. I wasn't one of the lads. I'd been waiting for Adrian to finally retire so I could get my chance, but when he was eventually pushed out, they gave the spot to another young, white Englishman. That's when I knew I was never going to be given the opportunity to show what I could really do."

"Is that why you started selling information about the players and your club to bookmakers?" asked Lynn.

Cliff licked his lips and gripped the perimeter rail so tightly his tendons stood out.

"We found an old article with the allegations," Dotty explained. "And I guess they're true. You were trying to make it in the cricketing world without the support from family or friends."

"Ain't that the truth," Cliff replied, relaxing a little. "I came here to make my name, but I had to survive. My wages barely covered the rent, let alone kit or any other expenses."

"So you found another way to support yourself," Dotty enquired.

Cliff let go of the rail and folded his arms across his chest.

"I had to live on something."

"What I don't understand," Lynn said thoughtfully, "is why, since you and Adrian clearly weren't friends, he offered you a job here. Now he has to see you every day."

"Oh, he loves it. Bossing me around and acting like he's doing me a favour. And I can't complain. I need the job, the money, and the little cottage that comes with it. And…" his voice trailed off.

"He's got something over you?" Dotty suggested.

Cliff pressed his lips together and said nothing.

Lynn narrowed her eyes. "Is that the only reason he gave you the job? To keep you under his thumb? Or do you know something about him? Something that could threaten his position as deputy headmaster here?"

Cliff's eyes widened before he pushed himself back against the rail.

Lynn gave a slight nod. Then she added, "Look, I'm not here to pry into your working relationship unless it's relevant to my investigation. So tell me, what does this have to do with Pip? You were the first person to recognise her from her cricketing days."

Cliff's mouth twitched into a modest grin. "People always said I was observant."

That might explain why he was paid for information, Dotty thought. But something about him unsettled her. He reminded her of people who stayed on the fringes, watching and listening, and then using what they picked up to cause trouble behind the scenes. Was Cliff like that?

"You should ask Adrian about Philippa," he added.

"I have," said Lynn, "and I might again. But right now, I'm asking you. Did Pip know you were selling information? Was she the one who tipped off the reporter?"

"Of course not!" Cliff burst out. "She'd never have done that."

"But she did know what you were doing?"

Cliff let out a short, dismissive laugh. "I don't know. Maybe. So what?"

"Because," Lynn said firmly, "her death might not have been an accident. And if she knew about your dealings, and if you're still involved..."

Cliff shifted uncomfortably where he was standing.

Dotty glanced down at his feet and noticed his smart white trainers with a grey tick symbol. They looked new. And expensive.

"You are, aren't you," she said thoughtfully. "Those trainers. They look brand new. I'm just not sure they're the kind of thing someone would usually wear to work. Not on a groundsman's salary."

Cliff's voice tightened. "I have to be smart for match days."

"But not that fashionable," argued Lynn, also eyeing his footwear.

Dotty gave Cliff a measured look.

But it was Lynn who pressed further. "If you're still selling information, and Pip realised that, she might have threatened to expose you. That gives you a motive."

"A motive?" Cliff exclaimed. Several people turned to stare. He lowered his voice and added, "A motive for what?"

"Harming Pip."

"But I thought ..."

"We can't confirm yet how she died. That's why I'm asking questions," Lynn said evenly.

Dotty added, "And maybe she wasn't the only one who suspected something. Perhaps that's why you ended up with this job."

Cliff tensed and looked round nervously.

"Oh, so Adrian gets a cut?" Lynn said, her voice cool. "Pip wouldn't have liked that. It was bad enough knowing you were supplementing your earnings, but for Adrian to profit too?" She let the thought hang in the air.

"She didn't know," Cliff muttered. "Not from me. And I'd never harm Philippa. She was the only one who ever encouraged me. The only one who told me I had something to offer and that I should keep training and ignore what others said. I wish I'd listened to her. I should've ignored players like Adrian. Maybe then I would've made it as a cricket star."

The memory seemed to lift him. He smiled for the first time. "And it was a joy seeing her out there again today. Striking the ball, taking wickets. Just like old times."

CHAPTER THIRTY-TWO

DOTTY

"Do you think Cliff could have killed Pip?" Lynn asked as she and Dotty made their way back to the members' pavilion.

"He could have done. Everything he told us about Pip, and even Adrian, might be a lie, but I don't think it is. He as good as admitted to selling information when he was a player, and he didn't deny still doing it now."

"Or that Adrian Cartwright knows and is taking a cut. He really is a weasel," muttered Lynn.

Dotty gasped. It was unlike the inspector to speak ill of anyone. But she did have a point.

"So what next?" asked Dotty.

"I think we should see if the Larks have unearthed any more interesting stories about our victim or suspects."

Keya and Sujin were nowhere to be seen when Dotty and Lynn returned.

"Inspector," Aunt Beanie called as she spotted them entering the members' pavilion.

"Have you found something else?" Lynn asked, approaching the table. Georgina sat up straighter, and Clara and Bryonie both nodded.

"I have," said Olivia proudly, tapping her phone.

"We've all been searching for the article Clare Savage wrote that implicated Pip and mentioned a 'business'," Aunt Beanie explained. "That's what Clare was referring to."

"There are quite a few articles," Georgina added.

"But I found the original," Olivia said, placing her phone on the table and smiling.

Lynn sat down. "Great. What does it say?"

Olivia hesitated.

"It's OK, just read out the same sections you read to us," Georgina encouraged.

Olivia took a breath, picked up her phone and began, "Goldcrest Sports Promotion shines like a beacon in the world of sports marketing, with star ambassadors like Gifford Rivers giving it the golden touch. But who really holds the purse strings? Behind the polished façade, ownership is murky, tangled in offshore accounts and silent investors. Could this high-profile company be hiding something far less glamorous?"

Olivia paused as Aunt Beanie commented, "Goldcrest must be the company Clare was talking about."

Olivia continued reading. "But it's not just Goldcrest's investors who have questions to answer. Rising star Philippa Lawson, already tipped as the future of women's cricket, played a key role in bringing Goldcrest into the sport's inner circle. Sources close to the company suggest that Lawson personally introduced Gifford Rivers to its directors, paving the way for lucrative sponsorship deals and promotional campaigns.

"While Rivers remains the face of Goldcrest's sporting ambitions, insiders now question just how deep Lawson's involvement runs. Is she merely a well-meaning intermediary, or does she have a vested interest in Goldcrest's expansion into English cricket? With speculation mounting over the company's financial dealings, one question looms large: does Philippa Lawson simply show poor judgement, or is she fully aware of the company she is keeping?"

"That certainly dumped Pip in it," Keya observed as she and Sujin joined the group.

Bryonie and Clara nodded.

Olivia smiled self-consciously and carried on reading. "Lawson and Rivers aren't just two of English cricket's most celebrated names, they are its most dazzling duo. Photographed at exclusive events, rubbing shoulders with sporting elites, and jetting off on luxury trips, they seem to have it all. But with Goldcrest Sports Promotion now under scrutiny, one question remains unanswered. Who is really footing the bill?

"Are these glamorous getaways and high-end parties simply the perks of rising fame, or is there more to the story? With Goldcrest's backers still shrouded in mystery, speculation is mounting over whether Rivers' and Lawson's gilded lifestyle is built on solid ground, or whether they are enjoying the spoils of a company whose riches may be tarnished."

Zach appeared at Dotty's side and wrapped an arm around her waist.

She smiled, enjoying the connection between them as Olivia continued. "When asked about his relationship to Goldcrest and its investors, Rivers is quick to defend himself, but his words do little to clear Lawson's name. 'I'm just the face of it. I do my job, promote the brand, and play my cricket. But Philippa? She introduced me to them, vouched for them. I trusted her judgement. If there is more going on, I have no idea.'

"With Rivers distancing himself from the deeper dealings, attention now turns to Lawson, the breakout star who introduced Goldcrest to the sport. Is she simply reckless in her associations, or does she know more than she is letting on? Once hailed as the future of women's cricket, Lawson now finds herself at the centre of a scandal that casts a long shadow over her career. And in a game where reputation is everything, redemption may prove far harder to secure than a sponsorship deal."

Olivia finished reading, her cheeks pink as she placed her phone back on the table.

"Wow," was all Dotty could say.

"I think that's called a hatchet job," Aunt Beanie declared.

"I'm disappointed in Gifford for not standing by her," Zach said.

"Lynn and I have just spoken to him. He was young back then, with his career ahead of him. And I suspect Clare twisted his words, or at least made them look worse than he intended," Dotty reflected. "He was sorry, wasn't he?" She looked at Lynn, who nodded thoughtfully.

"And I think he still loved her," Dotty added.

Zach tightened his hold on her waist, gently pulling her closer. "I would never do that," he whispered.

Dotty smiled at him gratefully, but as she turned back to the group, she saw that Mel and Tani had joined them. Mel, standing just behind Georgina, was staring at her coolly.

Zach might never intentionally hurt her. But then, Gifford probably hadn't meant to harm Pip either. And yet, some actions still had consequences.

CHAPTER THIRTY-THREE

DOTTY

Inspector Lynn Lockwood took a deep breath.

Dotty tried to calm her anxious thoughts about Zach and his admirer, Mel, as she went back over the article Olivia had read aloud and the implications it held for the investigation into Pip's death.

In essence, it claimed that Pip had introduced Gifford to a foreign company interested in investing in British cricket. Gifford had become the face of the company, giving it credibility, and in return, according to Clare Savage's article, some of the glamorous trips and events he and Pip had enjoyed were funded by the company.

But Clare had done more than raise questions. She had discredited Pip. Had that been necessary for the article, or were there personal motives at play?

"It's clear I need to speak to Clare Savage," Lynn said, resignation in her voice. "And this time, she'd better tell me everything." She glanced at Dotty and Aunt Beanie.

"Before you go," Keya said.

Everyone turned to look at her.

"We've had an update from the pathologist. Just preliminary findings from the external examination of Pip's wound. He isn't ruling out that she was killed by a cricket ball," Keya explained, "but he does agree with Dr Peters' initial thoughts that it was most likely a rectangular object that caused the damage to her skull. He'll know more after the internal examination."

"The cricket bat," concluded Lynn, nodding.

Dotty asked, "Did you find any fingerprints on it?"

Sujin replied, "Yes. I examined the handle and blade under a UV light. The string around the grip is dry and frayed, so prints there are hard to make out. On the rest of the bat, there are plenty, but many are smudged. Isolating the person who swung it will be tricky, but it might still be worth testing further if we can narrow down our pool of suspects."

"Which I'm trying to do," Lynn said with a sigh, glancing towards the front of the tent, where Emily was still sitting.

How long could Tilly entertain her, Dotty wondered, conscious of the warmth of Zach's arm still around her waist. What had Pip's relationship with Gifford really been like? And how must she have felt reading that article, believing he had betrayed her?

"You said there were more articles," Dotty prompted. "What do they say?"

Georgina tapped her phone. "The Herald Sports Extra wrote, 'Once the sport's golden couple, Rivers and Lawson now find themselves under fire. Not just for their ties to Goldcrest, but for the secrets that may have existed behind closed doors.' I think they're hinting at relationship troubles."

Bryonie chimed in. "The Daily Play said something similar." She read aloud, "Sources suggest the cracks began long before the scandal broke. Was Rivers already distancing himself from Lawson before the press uncovered Goldcrest's questionable dealings?"

"It must be hard to stay together when everyone around you is questioning your loyalty," Georgina remarked. "Even if you were committed, it would start to wear you down."

"Like a self-fulfilling prophecy," Lynn murmured.

Mel scrolled quickly, then said, "Here's a quote from an unnamed team member: 'He threw her under the bus, plain and simple. One moment they're presenting awards together, the next he's blaming her for everything. What happened to standing by your teammate?'"

"That sums it up very well. The betrayal," Aunt Beanie observed.

"This is all useful background," Lynn acknowledged, "but while it gave Pip a reason to hold a grudge or two, it still doesn't explain why anyone would want to harm her."

She looked at Dotty with a wry smile. "Fancy joining me for another chat with Clare Savage?"

"Of course," Dotty replied, then glanced at Zach. "You don't mind, do you?"

"No, of course not. You've been invited to help." A smile tugged at his lips. "Go on, then. Solve it, and then we can all go home."

"Hear, hear," Aunt Beanie chimed in.

Dotty was smiling as she left the members' pavilion, encouraged by the support of her friends. But as she turned to look back at Zach, she saw him deep in conversation with Mel. She was standing close, her body angled squarely towards him in a way that felt just a little too familiar.

A knot of doubt twisted in Dotty's stomach. Could he really mean what he'd said earlier, about never letting her down the way Gifford had with Pip? Or was she being naïve?

"He's just being friendly," Lynn said, as if reading Dotty's mind. "Do you want to go back?"

"No," Dotty replied firmly. Getting justice for Pip mattered more right now. She could talk to Zach later. Perhaps find something they could do together, something fun. Without any dead bodies.

As if sensing her thoughts, Zach looked up and smiled at her, and Dotty felt reassured.

Feeling steadier, she walked with Lynn towards the players' and officials' pavilion.

"First, we need to find Clare," Lynn said. "I doubt she'll return to the press room until after the match is finished."

CHAPTER THIRTY-FOUR

KEYA

Keya watched Dotty accompany Lynn out of the members' pavilion to speak to the reporter, Clare Savage. She hoped they might find some answers about the article Clare had written, and whether it did have any connection to Pip's death.

Turning to Sujin, she said, "It's interesting that Pip didn't take her husband's name."

"Many successful women don't. They've built their careers on their own names, and changing them could jeopardise what they've achieved." He gave her a thoughtful look. "Would you change your name when you marry?"

"Me?" she squawked, caught completely off guard. What was Sujin getting at?

"I just wondered," he said with a small smile. "You're independent, you've built a career and a business, and now you're forging a new path entirely on your own terms."

"I haven't really thought about it," she admitted. "What do you think?"

"I wouldn't mind either way."

A smile tugged at Keya's lips, but before she could say more, Sujin turned his head towards the entrance to the pavilion.

Members of the Coln Akeman Larks, seated at another table and chatting in low tones, also looked over as the unmistakable figure of Gifford Rivers strode towards them.

Tani ran a hand through her short dark hair, pushed back her chair, and stood up. But Gifford's focus was on the empty wooden frame where the bat he'd recently purchased had been displayed. He walked past the Larks with a puzzled expression, ignoring Tani's coy, "Hi, Gifford."

Keya and Sujin followed him to the display. After several seconds of silent staring, Gifford's gaze dropped to the floor.

Sujin cleared his throat. "If you're looking for your bat, I'm afraid it's not here."

"Where is it? I paid a lot of money for that bat. Don't tell me someone used it to play cricket and broke it." His shoulders sagged and he pressed his lips together.

"Actually, it's surprisingly sturdy," Sujin said lightly. "And don't worry, we have it."

Gifford frowned, clearly puzzled. "Can I have it back? I need to return to the commentary box before the end of the match."

"I can certainly show it to you," Sujin said, gesturing for Gifford to accompany him.

Keya suspected Sujin was deliberately drawing him away from the bar and tea area to talk in private.

At their table, Sujin picked up a large brown bag. Part of the handle and the flat face of the bat were visible through a transparent panel.

"Why on earth have you put it in that? Can I have it back now?" Gifford's brow furrowed as he repeated his previous question.

"I'm sorry," Keya said. "It's going to be sent to the lab for forensic examination."

"It's just a cricket bat. An old one, sure, but it's signed by Bradman and his Invincibles. You'll ruin it with your tests. What's the point?"

"It's evidence," Keya replied evenly.

"Evidence of what?" His voice rose sharply.

Keya glanced at Sujin, who gave a small nod.

"A potential murder."

Gifford paled. His mouth opened slightly before he managed, "Who else is dead?"

"Nobody else, Mr Rivers," Sujin said firmly. "We are formally treating Philippa Lawson's death as suspicious."

"But... but... the cricket ball."

"That's what we all thought," Keya said. "But the evidence suggests she may have been struck by something else. Your cricket bat."

"But I'd never strike Philippa!" Gifford looked horrified, as he took a step back.

They waited, giving him a moment to absorb the shock.

Finally, he said quietly, "You think she was murdered."

"We have to work on that presumption until the evidence proves otherwise," Sujin explained.

"So that's why you've been asking all those questions. And now I'm a suspect?"

"Anyone from her past who's here today is being interviewed," Keya replied, her tone neutral.

Gifford shook his head slowly. "This just keeps getting worse. I was thrilled to see her bowl again. Then I found out she had a partner, which, honestly, shouldn't have surprised me. She was attractive, brilliant. And now... she's gone. And you're saying someone might have killed her. I don't know how to process this."

"Here, have a seat," Keya said quickly.

Gifford sank onto the nearest chair, his hands resting on his knees. He looked stunned.

Tani appeared beside him. "Can I help you?" she asked, her voice soft.

"Some water would be good," Keya replied, trying to keep the irritation out of her voice. Now was hardly the time for Tani to be flirting.

Tani didn't respond to her but kept her eyes on Gifford.

He looked up. "Yes. Water. I'd appreciate that."

"Of course you would," Tani said with a sigh and headed to the bar. As she walked away, she gave a subtle thumbs up to someone at the Larks' table.

Keya followed her gaze and frowned.

Mel had positioned herself in front of Zach. The two were standing near the Larks' table, and Mel touched Zach's lapel as she said, "I really enjoyed our drink last week. We should do it again."

"I'm sure we will. Although after Pip's death, now doesn't feel like the right time to celebrate. Maybe in a couple of weeks. I'll speak to Sujin. Perhaps we could all go out."

Mel tilted her head. "Or just the two of us. For a quiet drink."

"I don't think that would be appropriate," Zach said, taking a step back.

Mel stepped forward. "But you said you liked me. You weren't lying, were you?"

"No. Of course not," Zach said quickly. "And I do like you. As a friend."

Mel twisted a hoop earring between her fingers. "Friend! Oh, I think it's more than that."

Before Zach could react, Mel grabbed his face and kissed him.

"Zach!" cried a distraught high-pitched voice.

Keya spun round. Her chest tightened as she saw Dotty standing at the edge of the pavilion, pale, wide-eyed and frozen. Then her friend turned and rushed out of the members' pavilion.

Without hesitating, Keya took off after her.

CHAPTER THIRTY-FIVE

DOTTY: TEN MINUTES EARLIER

After five minutes of searching, Lynn and Dotty finally discovered Clare Savage in a narrow gap between two stands, where she had a player backed into a corner.

He looked visibly relieved at the sight of them and, seizing Clare's momentary distraction, ducked under her arm and made a swift escape.

Clare pursed her lips in dissatisfaction as she watched him retreat.

"I was sure I was onto a good story there. And then you two barged in and ruined it. I've already spoken to you. What do you want now?" she asked rudely.

"Perhaps you'd prefer to accompany me to Cirencester police station, where I can conduct a formal interview?" Lynn said coolly.

"I hardly think that's necessary," Clare replied quickly, her voice rising in pitch.

"Then you won't mind answering a few follow-up questions now," Lynn said smoothly. "In particular, about the article you wrote on Goldcrest Sports Promotions, and your suggestion that Pip was involved in some form of impropriety."

"Impropriety is a strong word," Clare said with a shrug, although her eyes were watchful. "I simply pointed out a few interesting links. It wasn't exactly investigative journalism."

"But what you wrote broke up Pip and Gifford's relationship," Dotty pointed out.

"How do you know? Is that what Gifford told you?" Clare scoffed. "All this talk about what a fantastic couple they were, but I knew better," she added with a dismissive tone.

"Really?" Lynn raised an eyebrow. "And what exactly did you know?"

Clare hesitated. For once, she seemed unsure how to respond. She was used to asking difficult questions, not having to answer them. She shifted uncomfortably.

"You see," Lynn continued, "I think Gifford had strong feelings for Pip. That he still does. Were you jealous?"

"I..." Clare faltered.

But Lynn pressed on. "I can't help wondering if what you wrote was just speculation, or even lies, designed to cause a rift between them. And speaking of lies, why didn't you tell the truth about where you were after the prize-giving? You denied speaking to Pip."

Clare seemed to recover some of her self-assurance and arrogance as she said offhandedly, "I might have said a few words. Congratulated her on her winning return. That sort of thing."

"That doesn't match what our witness described. They said Pip was angry. That she accused you of twisting the truth and blaming her for something. The claims in your article, I presume."

"You'd think she'd be over that by now, wouldn't you?" Clare exclaimed. "It's been fifteen years."

"Fifteen years away from the world she loved," Dotty stressed. She didn't add, and the man she loved, because she couldn't know for certain, but it felt likely.

Clare crossed her arms and stuck out her chin. She was clearly rattled.

Lynn pressed on. "And that wasn't the only time you spoke to Pip. You went back after Gifford talked to her."

"So Gifford's the one who spilled. Typical. That man never had any backbone. So what if I went back to speak to Philippa?"

"So what? Because her turning up today might have unsettled you. Was there something she knew that you didn't want brought up again?

Something questionable, like going through someone's property without permission?"

Clare pulled in her chin and shifted her stance.

"Or impersonating someone to get information. Or offering money for access."

Clare stiffened. "Now wait a minute. I've never bribed anyone," she said sharply.

Dotty couldn't tell whether Lynn was bluffing, but Clare hadn't denied the other points.

"Or perhaps you crossed what Pip saw as a moral line. Maybe you broke her trust."

Clare pressed her lips together and looked distinctly uncomfortable.

Lynn gave a slow nod. "I suspect it was a bit of everything. And that would have hurt Pip, especially if she still considered you a friend."

"You have no idea what it was like back then," Clare snapped. "Trying to break into sports journalism as an unknown woman from outside London. If you weren't from the right school or the right postcode, you were invisible."

She paused, then pressed on, her voice still tight with frustration. "What I wrote about Goldcrest was true. They did have shady backers. And they pulled out of cricket, and vanished from the sports scene in the UK only a few months after my article was published. I'm convinced they were laundering money. Why else would they walk away after investing so much just because a few questions were being asked?"

She relaxed and shook her head. "I meant to say how sorry I was. To apologise. But Philippa just made me feel worse. And when that happens, I become all defensive and angry. It wasn't how I meant it to happen."

Finally, Dotty thought, they were beginning to see the real Clare. The one full of doubts and insecurities, who used abrasive behaviour to mask a lack of confidence as she tried to break into a competitive and cut-throat profession.

"Were you in love with Gifford?" Dotty asked gently.

Clare sighed. "I know that's what a lot of people thought at the time. But no, not him."

"Someone else?" Lynn suggested, unable to hide her curiosity.

Clare's arms dropped to her sides. "Yes," she admitted reluctantly.

Dotty wondered who. Was it someone she'd already met in the cricketing world?

Lynn asked simply, "What happened?"

"He put his cricketing career first," Clare said, her voice quieter now. "And then when that floundered, he turned to less honest means of making a living. I knew, of course. And I should have exposed him, but I didn't. Not even when the rumours started, nor when he kept confiding in Pip instead of me."

She looked up at them, her voice tight. "I think he might have been in love with her. And perhaps I did hold a grudge about that. Maybe it's one of the reasons I was so vocal about her involvement with Goldcrest. After the article came out, she asked why I'd done it. Why incriminate her when she'd done nothing, and said nothing, about Clifford's dealings."

"Clifford? As in Cliff the groundsman here?" Lynn tried to hide the incredulous note in her voice.

But the surprise seemed to help ease the tension.

Clare laughed. "I know. He doesn't look like much now. The years have been hard on him. But when he arrived, he was this bright, colourful character with an exotic background. I was immediately drawn to him."

She paused, then looked at each of them in turn before continuing more softly.

"And if you must know, it was him, Cliff, that Pip and I talked about when I went back to speak to her. She said she couldn't believe we were both still single and told me she'd finally found love again with Ned, and asked why I didn't give it another try. She admitted Ned didn't have the looks, excitement or passion of Gifford, but he was reliable and dependable, which was more than she could say for most people in her life. She admitted to being content, living quietly in the Cotswolds. And even after everything, she told me she hoped I'd find love and peace too."

Dotty thought she saw a tear glisten at the corner of Clare's eye. But

Clare sniffed, turned away briefly, and when she faced them again, her composure had returned.

"And maybe I will," she said. "A legacy to Philippa. So you can believe me when I say, I felt no ill will. We parted, if not as friends, then at least on civil terms. And after what happened, that is a huge relief to me."

Dotty believed her. And she was glad they'd had the chance to make peace.

"One final question," Lynn said. "Did you see where Pip went after you finished speaking to her?"

"Yes. She was with Ned. He joined us just after she urged me to speak to Clifford."

Clare hesitated, frowning. "And I can see what she meant about dependable, although there was a look about him. A flicker of something behind the eyes I couldn't quite place, but perhaps I was just imagining it."

She glanced off into the distance, before adding, "And then they left. And so did I. I wanted to find out what Gifford was doing in the sponsors' tents and whether he'd comment on Philippa's reappearance."

"And that was the last time you saw her?" Lynn asked.

Clare nodded, her expression subdued. "I'm afraid so."

CHAPTER THIRTY-SIX

DOTTY

Dotty and Lynn walked with a despondent-looking Clare towards the boundary of the cricket field.

"Gloucestershire only need two more wickets," Clare said, glancing at the scoreboard. Her tone was neutral, lacking the excitement and tension that now rippled through the crowd.

All around them, spectators were murmuring, shifting in their seats, and willing the home team to win.

Dotty suspected Clare was clinging to the cricket to avoid facing the emotional weight of the day. But then Clare glanced to her right.

Cliff was leaning against the perimeter rail, his arms folded as he watched the match. As if sensing her presence, he turned and his gaze locked with Clare's. Hostility flared in his eyes, which gave way to surprise, and then softened into a guarded smile.

"Excuse me," Clare murmured, and without another word, she walked towards Cliff.

Dotty and Lynn headed in the opposite direction, weaving back through the crowd towards the members' pavilion.

"Perhaps something good can come from today," Lynn said, in a cautiously optimistic tone.

"Let's hope so," Dotty replied. "And if Clare and Cliff can make a go of things, maybe she'll soften a little, and stop hunting for flaws in everyone and instead start looking for the good in people."

"I wouldn't go that far," Lynn chuckled. Then she took a breath and added, "OK. What next?"

Dotty sensed it was a rhetorical question and she didn't answer.

"I think I need to speak to Adrian Cartwright again," Lynn continued. "He's the one person I can see who truly had a reason to hurt Pip."

"Because she left him for Gifford?" Dotty asked.

"Yes. But I think it's more than just resentment. Adrian craves control. You can see it in the way he treats Cliff. It's all about feeling superior. When Pip disappeared, he lost that control over her. But then she reappears, and with a new partner. Since they're still legally married, I think he saw a chance to reassert his power over her."

"But isn't the situation the same as with the other suspects? Pip had more reason to resent Adrian than he did to resent her."

"Maybe," Lynn said slowly. "But if Pip stood up to Adrian, if she challenged him, then he wouldn't have liked that one bit."

"Oh." Dotty paused as they reached the entrance to the members' pavilion. "I see what you mean."

Lynn walked ahead of her, and Dotty noticed Keya and Sujin standing at the table they had claimed earlier, with Tani beside them. And was that Gifford sitting down?

Tani looked smug, and as she turned and moved away she glanced across at … Mel.

Dotty froze.

Mel and Zach were standing very close together, speaking … intimately.

And as she watched in disbelief, Mel reached up, took hold of Zach's head, and pulled him towards her.

They kissed.

Dotty gasped and let out a soft cry.

How could Zach do that to her, after everything he'd said?

She couldn't believe it.

She had to get away.

She couldn't watch any more.

Fleeing from the members' pavilion, she heard someone call out, "Dotty."

But she kept walking.

CHAPTER THIRTY-SEVEN

KEYA

"Dotty," Keya called as she jogged to catch up with her friend. "It isn't what it looks like."

Dotty stopped and turned to face her, tears running down her cheeks.

"Don't lie to me. I saw everything."

"Not Zach's face. Or the way he froze with shock and struggled to break free from Mel."

"He didn't look like he was struggling to me."

"No, because you turned and scarpered before he had a chance to. You know how Mel's been with him. He was just trying to be friendly."

"A bit too friendly," Dotty protested, but she sounded defensive rather than angry.

"Please, don't let this ruin things. It's been a stressful day, and all our nerves are frayed. If only we could tie up this case and give Pip, and ourselves, some closure before we all go home. Come back with me."

An eruption of applause and cheers broke out around them as music blared from the nearby tannoys.

"Gloucestershire only need one more wicket," Dotty said in a small voice as Keya led her back to the members' pavilion.

Keya was relieved her friend had calmed down, but she asked, "How do you know that? I've no idea what's been happening in this match."

"Clare Savage told us the home side only needed two more wickets to win, and I presume they've just taken one of them."

"I take it she isn't our culprit, since you haven't returned with her in handcuffs?"

Dotty shook her head and wiped her glistening eyes with the sleeve of her short, neat jacket.

"No. Although she and Pip had harsh words, I think they made their peace before Pip died."

"That's good, but it leaves us without a prime suspect."

"Lynn thinks Adrian might have done it, especially if he tried to exert control over Pip again and she pushed back. He wouldn't have liked that."

"No, I'm sure you're right," Keya agreed, as they re-entered the members' pavilion.

Dotty glanced around quickly.

Keya couldn't see Mel.

"I sent them away," Aunt Beanie called out.

"Who?" Keya asked, walking towards the table where the other Larks were still sitting.

"Mel, for that disgusting behaviour with Zach. And Tani, as she was flirting with Gifford. So inappropriate. Look at the poor man."

Keya turned her head and saw Sujin smile sympathetically. Gifford was facing him, slumped forward in another chair.

Lynn approached Gifford and said, "I realise this is a shock, but can I ask you a few questions about your cricket bat?"

Gifford looked up, his face pale and drawn. He was without his usual energy and charm. But perhaps this was the real Gifford. The one Pip had fallen in love with.

Keya sighed at the sadness of it all as Gifford nodded slowly.

Lynn placed another chair beside Sujin's and asked, "Why did you bring the cricket bat today?"

"It wasn't to kill Philippa," Gifford blurted out.

"I know that," Lynn said gently. "But it does seem a bit odd hanging an old cricket bat up in a tent."

"It's not just any bat. And besides, I thought the members would appreciate seeing it. They love a bit of cricketing history."

Lynn nodded, although Keya wasn't sure she accepted the explanation.

"And when did you last see it?"

"That would be..." Gifford paused. "Between the end of the women's match and their prize-giving. I popped back to grab a drink and something to eat. I'd been speaking in the sponsors' tents over lunch. One of the members had seen me hang the bat in its frame and asked about it. A few others gathered round, and we had a good chat before I left for the prize-giving."

"Did it stay in the frame during that whole time?"

"No, I took it out and passed it round. And I wasn't the only one who had done that. I noticed one of the clips was bent, so someone must have removed it earlier."

"But you didn't see who?"

"No. I was busy. Harriet had asked me to introduce and commentate on the women's final. She said it would make the match feel more prestigious, and attract more attention."

"How noble of you, Gifford," came a sneering voice. "Lending your voice to the novelty of the women's match. Must have been quite the come down from the red carpets and rooftop bars."

Adrian Cartwright had arrived, unnoticed until that moment.

Keya's focus remained on Gifford. She waited for his cutting, witty retort, but instead he responded calmly, his voice sincere.

"Cricket is a sport for everyone, no matter their gender, colour, background or level. This morning's match was just as exciting as any county game I've covered. There was real passion. And the players' emotions were authentic."

"Like yours when you saw Philippa?" Adrian's voice sharpened. "Who were you trying to kid, lifting her up and spinning her round? What a disgusting display of public affection." He took a step closer, anger rising with each word. "After everything. You were the one who sold her out. The one who made her disappear. Who drove her from me, from cricket, from her life."

"You're right," Gifford said quietly. "I should never have let Philippa take the blame for my involvement with Goldcrest. She didn't know any more about their background than I did. They seemed legitimate to both of us, and we were impressed. They genuinely appeared to want to invest in cricket. They had money to splash around. And let's face it... I was flattered."

"But you were quoted as blaming Pip," said Lynn, still seated opposite Gifford. She was letting Adrian's unfiltered outbursts channel her interview.

"Clare took that out of context. She betrayed us both. I thought we were having a conversation about how Philippa and I had both been deceived by Goldcrest. I even asked her advice about how to walk away if what she'd found out was true."

"You always were an idiot," Adrian snapped.

Gifford gave him a cool look, before turning back to Lynn.

"But that was one thing I didn't have to worry about. By the end of the season, Goldcrest were gone. They pulled out of the UK as soon as the authorities began looking into them. But by then... I'd already lost Philippa."

"Oh, poor Gifford," Adrian sneered. "Did you have to learn to stand on your own two feet?"

Gifford leaned back slightly and looked steadily up at him. "Do you ever wonder why she left you? Why she ran from you and came to me? A man you clearly despise."

"She didn't run," Adrian said flatly. "She was a silly little girl who didn't get her way. She thought you could give her what she wanted. But you were a boy, not a man. And she was a fool to trust you. I told her as much. And look what happened."

Gifford rose slowly to his feet and turned to face Adrian. They were both tall, but Gifford had the advantage of both height and presence. He'd kept his firm, athletic build, while Adrian looked plump and out of shape. Keya suspected he relied on his sharp brain and even sharper tongue to put people in their place.

"You can't do it, can you?" Gifford said, his voice steady but low. "Admit what a vile, narcissistic man you really are." He took a step closer.

Adrian stiffened, ready to retaliate, but Gifford spoke first.

"Philippa was only nineteen when she married you. A father figure. Someone who should have guided and supported her. But instead, you belittled her, constantly undermining her ambition and her confidence." He shook his head in disgust.

Adrian's face darkened.

Gifford tilted his head slightly and added, coolly, "What was it, Adrian? Couldn't you bear the thought that she—your wife—might have more talent than you? And be more popular? Your career only lasted as long as it did because you were married to Philippa."

Adrian's nostrils flared and his jaw twitched. Without a word, he shoved Gifford squarely in the chest, forcing him back a step.

But Gifford didn't flinch. He steadied himself and stared at Adrian, fists clenched at his sides.

"Go on," he said quietly. "Throw your weight around. That's what you do, isn't it? Dominate. Intimidate. Hurt. But this time, you picked someone your own size. Someone who can fight back."

Keya held her breath.

The two men locked eyes.

Who would move first?

"That's enough," said a voice which was both firm and level.

The tension cracked. Everyone blinked.

Keya's mouth fell open.

Ned stood between the two taller men, one arm pressed firmly against Gifford's chest, the other raised towards Adrian. His voice was calm, but it carried an unexpected authority.

"This isn't about either of you. And it won't help her now."

Gifford took a step back, while Adrian, still breathing hard, looked momentarily thrown.

Keya watched, surprised. This wasn't the quiet, bookish man she thought she knew.

Adrian recovered first and scoffed, "So, the replacement finally speaks. I thought you were too dull to have an opinion. Earlier, bleating on about how proud you'd be to work at Ashcombe Manor, and inspire the pupils with your soft little English teacher skills." He gave a sharp, scornful laugh. "I wouldn't hire you if you were the last teacher in the county. You stupid, pathetic little man."

Wham.

Adrian hit the floor.

CHAPTER THIRTY-EIGHT

DOTTY

Dotty jumped.

She hadn't seen that coming.

Nor had she thought of Ned as dull, the way Adrian had, rather more… harmless.

Sujin squatted beside Adrian and asked, "Are you all right down there?"

"Of course I am. I just… tripped, that's all. Give me a hand up."

Sujin stood and pulled Adrian to his feet.

Lynn, Gifford, and the group of Larks all watched in silence.

"That's quite a mark on your cheek," Sujin noted. "You'll have a sizeable bruise. The cut on your lip isn't deep, but it must be sore."

"It's not. I'm fine. Stop fussing." Adrian brushed down his navy blazer and straightened his tie. Only then did he seem to notice everyone staring at him.

"Enjoying the show?" he muttered, struggling to sound composed, before turning on his heel and hurrying away.

Lynn had observed the scene with quiet interest, but Adrian's sudden retreat caught her off guard. She moved quickly, calling after him, "Mr Cartwright. Can I have a word?"

"That's quite a right hook you've got," said Gifford to Ned, his tone a mix of admiration and amusement. The jovial, energetic Gifford Dotty knew was beginning to return.

"I... I didn't mean to hit him," Ned stammered.

"But he pushed all the right buttons?" Gifford suggested.

"I didn't care what he said about me. I'm used to that. I've had harsher comments from my pupils," he added with a wry smile. "But Pip... after everything I've learned today about her marriage, and how he treated her... I just lost control."

Ned seemed genuinely remorseful.

"Well, I think he deserved it," declared Aunt Beanie. "What an odious, vile man. Well done, Ned."

Ned blushed just as Lynn rejoined the group.

"I agree with Bernadette," she said. "And I'd love to pin this murder on him, but he says he was with the officials from the end of the prize-giving well into the start of the county game. We'll check, of course, but despite him having the clearest motive, I'm inclined to believe he had nothing to do with Pip's death."

Ned walked around the table to stand beside Lynn, Dotty, and Keya.

His voice was heavy with concern. "Did you say murder? Of Pip?"

"I'm afraid so," Lynn said. "That's the view of both the examining doctor and the pathologist. It wasn't the cricket ball that killed her, it was a cricket bat."

"Oh no." Ned grabbed the back of a chair for support.

"I'm sorry," Lynn added gently. "And I didn't mean for you to find out like this."

"Come and sit with us," Aunt Beanie suggested kindly.

As Lynn helped Ned to an empty seat, Dotty considered what she'd said about Adrian's alibi, particularly the timing.

Turning to Keya, she asked, "Do you know when Pip was killed?"

"Dr Peter couldn't be that precise, but he said within an hour of finding her body, probably less."

Dotty nodded. "And Harriet said she was alive when the county match was starting, as the players were being announced. That's when she rushed off, leaving Pip and Ned together."

Dotty glanced towards Ned, who was speaking quietly to Aunt Beanie.

"And Gifford had an alibi for that time. He was in the sponsors' tent, giving a talk, and several people confirmed it. Adrian says he was with the officials. There's nobody to vouch for Clare, but she doesn't seem to have a motive, and I believed her when she said she and Pip made up. Cliff, the groundsman, could move around as he pleased, although I'm not sure he'd easily have gained easy access to the members' pavilion, but he might have blagged his way in."

"What reason would he have to kill Pip?" asked Keya, surprised.

"None, really. He knew her from her cricketing days and said they were friends. He used to sell information for money, and he probably still does, but I doubt Pip had a chance to find out about that. And even if she did, I'm not sure he'd have resorted to violence to keep her quiet. Although..." Dotty's words trailed off, as she continued watching Ned and Aunt Beanie.

Then she asked, "Aren't we always drawn to the loud ones? Men like Adrian who throw their weight around. Who do their best to appear guilty. They bluster, they lie and, quite often, as Lynn said, we want them to be guilty. But how often are they?"

Keya sighed. "Fewer times than you think. It's often the quieter ones—the ones who hide in the background, the ones we overlook—who are actually guilty. They're just better at concealing it. And at hiding their emotions."

"Like Ned," Dotty said slowly.

"Yes, people like him," Keya agreed lightly. Then she turned and stared at Dotty, her eyes widening as understanding dawned.

"You mean actually like Ned, don't you?"

"Shush," murmured Dotty, drawing Keya away from the table where the Coln Akeman Larks were sitting.

Lynn followed, and when they stopped a safe distance away from the others, she asked, "What have you two worked out?"

"Ask Dotty. I'm still not entirely with her."

Dotty felt herself blush as both Keya and Lynn regarded her with quiet intent.

Taking a deep breath, she said, "We've been speaking to people Pip knew from her cricketing days. We've discovered that Adrian was an abusive husband, and that she left him for Gifford. But he, or at least Clare implied that he sold her out over the shady dealings with

Goldcrest, the foreign sports company. But what if this has more to do with the present than the past?" She glanced over at Ned and Aunt Beanie.

"Ned?" Lynn questioned, sounding sceptical.

"He was the last person anyone saw with Pip, at least according to Harriet. And we all thought he was mild-mannered. We know he doted on Pip and encouraged her to play cricket, but then..."

"He lashed out and hit Adrian. That was a surprise," Keya agreed.

"But why?" asked Lynn. "What motive would he have?"

"I'm not sure he did. Nothing about this crime feels premeditated. I think he just snapped, like he did with Adrian."

"And the cricket bat?" Lynn sounded unconvinced. "He had no reason to be holding it. How does that fit in?"

"I admit, I haven't worked that part out yet." Dotty looked at Keya and asked, "Could Ned have used the bat in self-defence? I wondered earlier if Gifford might have done so, but now I think that's unlikely."

"It's plausible," Keya said, though she sounded doubtful.

Lynn frowned. "I see where you're going, and yes, Ned punching Adrian caught us all by surprise. But to strike Pip? With that bat?"

Dotty shrugged, but her certainty grew, despite Lynn's doubts. She didn't want Ned to be the one who'd killed Pip. But she owed it to the quiet, unassuming woman who'd reluctantly stepped in to join the village team to find out. To the one who'd re-entered a world she'd tried so hard to leave behind. Pip was the one who deserved the truth.

"We'll just have to find out," said Dotty resolutely.

Keya gave her a doubtful look. "How?"

Dotty didn't reply straight away but her gaze rested on Ned.

He was alone now, sitting at the same table as Sujin, but turned slightly away from him. And he was staring ... at nothing.

"It has to come from him," Dotty said at last. "Ned needs to tell us."

Keya frowned. "Confessions don't just happen."

Dotty nodded. "I know it's a long shot. But we're all tired, and emotionally drained. So is Ned. If he did kill Pip, he must be weighed down by guilt. I'm not saying we pressure him with threats or accusations. But if we can persuade him to unburden himself. To admit what happened... it might give us all closure."

Lynn shrugged. "I'm out of any better ideas. If you think you can get to the truth, go ahead. I'll back you up."

Dotty nodded, then walked slowly towards Ned.

CHAPTER THIRTY-NINE

DOTTY

Ned looked up as Dotty approached him.

"When do you think the police will let me go home?" he asked.

"I guess when they've gathered as much information about Pip's case as they can, but it would be much easier for all of us if we knew what really happened and Pip's death was resolved. I know I'll sleep better tonight knowing that. Won't you?" she asked gently.

"I'm not sure when I'll ever be able to sleep again. Or live, for that matter. She was my world, you know."

Dotty slowly pulled out a chair and turned it to face Ned before she sat down. This felt like a promising start. She tried to set aside the fact that this was a police enquiry, and that Lynn was watching, and instead focus on the man in front of her. If she could help him, and ease his grief, perhaps it would lead to the truth and ultimately solve the case.

"I know. I saw that the first day we met, after Keya had hit me on the head with her bowling. You and Pip looked so content strolling around the village cricket field with your little terrier."

"I remember," mused Ned. "It was a wonderful evening. So warm, and with the calls of your team and the sound of bats hitting balls. An idyllic scene."

"And Pip was happy, wasn't she?"

"I hope so, although I can't help questioning that now. Like I'll question everything about our life together. I just don't understand. Why did she feel the need to lie to me?"

"About what?" Dotty pressed gently. She felt this was important.

"Her old life. The one everyone here seems to know about." Ned sounded bitter.

"I didn't, and nor did the rest of the Larks. We knew her as you did. A resident of Coln Akeman and a member of the women's cricket team."

"But your young man," pressed Ned, sounding more intense as he glanced up at Zach. He and Sujin were now standing with Keya and Lynn, talking in low tones. Lynn gave Dotty a questioning look, and then Zach gave her a reassuring smile.

"You haven't lied to him, have you?"

Dotty thought through her answer carefully before responding, "No, but he doesn't know all the details about my previous life. He does know I was married to a soldier and that he died, but the details of that marriage..."

Dotty shivered, not wanting to go there right now. "Those I haven't shared with him. I've put that part of my life behind me. I don't want to revisit it."

Then, holding Ned's gaze, she said, "And I don't believe Pip did either. She'd done everything she could to leave behind a past which caused her a great deal of pain and misery."

"But I could have helped her," protested Ned.

"You did help her. By being you. By being supportive and reliable, and enjoying the simple pleasures, such as walking your dog together on a balmy summer evening."

"You think that was enough for her? After the life she had in cricket? Being adored by fans and fawned over by officials and treated like royalty?"

"I do," Dotty replied. "Of course, coming here would have reawakened old memories and feelings. Some would have been enjoyable, like batting with Zivah, and taking those wickets to help her team to victory. Because I'm sure that's what really delighted her. Being a member of the team. And it didn't matter that we're a bunch of amateurs. She was part of a community. And so were you. Like me and Zach. We're all friends."

Dotty looked over at the Coln Akeman Larks.

When she turned back to Ned, she said, "But much of today would have been painful for her. She was very brave to come, and again, I think she did it because she didn't want to let the team down."

Ned nodded. "All those little things... like taking ages to pack, misplacing her shoes, pretending she wasn't feeling well. I see it now. She was stalling. I was the one who persuaded her to come. Because, as you said, I didn't want to let the village down. We both knew how hard everyone had worked, and reaching the final was such a huge achievement. But I should never have pushed her. I wouldn't have, not if I'd known. If only she'd told me."

His eyes widened, pleading. "Why didn't she?"

Dotty presumed he was referring to Pip's old life again.

"Because, as I said, that was in the past. We don't return to our childhood. It becomes a part of us. Something that shapes and influences us. Something we learn from. But then we move on. And that's what Pip had done. She'd moved on. To live her life. With you."

Ned sat back. "I couldn't see that. I'm still not sure. With all this..."

At that moment, the cricket ground erupted with applause, cheers and jubilant music from the speakers.

The commentator announced, "Congratulations to Gloucestershire on their convincing win."

"Pip didn't want all this," Dotty said a little louder so he could hear her over the celebrations. "Maybe when she was starting out, but not now. Sport is for the young. Look at Gifford. He was a star player once, but not anymore. He's had to find a new life outside cricket."

Ned did look at Gifford. But with envy, jealousy, and bitterness.

Dotty's eyes narrowed. "You thought Pip would leave you for him, didn't you?"

Still staring at Gifford, Ned nodded. "She'd have been a fool not to. He clearly still had feelings for her. And look at him. He's got the looks, the muscles, the charm. And what do I have?"

"You had Pip's trust. You hadn't let her down as he did. Even if Gifford told her that his words were twisted by the press, and that he regretted what happened, he still didn't protect her. He put his career first. And while Pip might, in time, have moved past it, I doubt she'd ever truly have forgiven him."

"But…" Ned faltered, struggling for words. His face twisted in confusion.

"I know it's hard to see clearly right now. Your world's been upended. You've learned things you didn't expect, and you're hurt. That's natural. It takes time to process. But the problem is, when emotions run high, we react. The old fight-or-flight response."

Dotty's words hung between them.

She glanced at Lynn, who gave her a questioning look.

"I…" Ned began, and Dotty returned her focus to him. But he seemed unable to continue.

She realised she had to tread carefully. He might need a little prompting, a gentle nudge in the right direction, but if she said or did too much he might clam up.

"I was upset. And I admit, rather overwhelmed. The team winning the match was fantastic. Everyone in Coln Akeman has been so welcoming since we arrived, and we've loved living there. But the way everyone talked about Pip. It was as if she was a different person." He stopped.

"That's a very thoughtful way of putting it. I think she probably was a different person in her cricketing days. Perhaps more impulsive and idealistic. But she was much younger then," Dotty ventured.

"But she'd been famous. And now all these people wanted to know her again. To be part of her life." He gave Gifford a quick glance. "To be part of our life."

Dotty's voice dropped to a whisper. "And you didn't want that. You wanted Pip all to yourself."

Ned nodded, looking down. "That was selfish of me, wasn't it?"

"No. It's understandable. And perhaps more than that. Your instinct was to protect her." Dotty said, although she suspected Ned was being more honest, and he had acted in his own self-interest.

"No, it wasn't," Ned admitted. "But then, maybe I did want to shield her. I knew she was upset. And Adrian…" He shook his head. "He pretended to be my friend. Showed me round the grounds. Brought me in here for a coffee. Showed me the cricket bat hanging on the wall. Was he using it to goad me? Toying with me, like a mouse?

Because he knew who Pip really was. That she was still his wife. And that meant she couldn't be mine."

"Had you and Pip talked about marriage?" Dotty asked gently.

"A couple of times. But she'd always been evasive. I understand why now. She was deceiving me." Ned's voice rose, bitter and wounded.

Dotty could hear the resentment. The soft approach hadn't worked. Maybe it was time for Ned to let the anger out.

She gave him a moment, and then asked softly, "Did that make you angry?"

"Of course it did. All our plans. All the things we'd talked about..."

"And now you'd have to share her. With the cricketing world. With people like Harriet Wintle."

"Oh, she couldn't stop gushing. She brought us into the members' pavilion, and all her cronies were fawning over Pip. Taking photographs of her with that bat. And that's when I realised. Adrian told me how Gifford had cheated him out of it. Said the bat was old, no longer playable, but people still wanted it. Admired it. Stared at it. Just like they were going to do with Pip. Harriet was already talking about meetings, speaking engagements, joining boards. She wanted control of Pip. To parade her around."

"To take her away from you?" Dotty suggested quietly, fuelling the fire.

"Exactly!" Ned exclaimed.

Dotty didn't glance at Lynn or Keya. She kept her focus entirely on Ned.

"They all did."

"You saw the way Gifford greeted Pip?" raised Dotty.

"Of course I did. How could I miss it? And I saw them together later. He was pleading with her. I know he wanted her back. He was trying to steal her away from me."

He stared at Gifford now with undisguised hatred.

"And did you say that to her, in here, after Harriet left? Did you confront her about leaving you?"

"I did. But of course, she denied it. Said I was more of a man than Gifford." He shook his head, frustrated.

"You didn't believe her."

"No. I grabbed the bat and held it in front of her. Said she'd always belong to cricket. Just like that old bat."

"And how did she respond?"

"She told me she didn't want that. That she had no interest in Harriet's charities or events. That cricket had turned its back on her. And she had nothing to give it anymore." He paused, his jaw tight. "But when she mentioned Gifford… her face changed. I saw how she really felt about him."

There was no mistaking the bitterness in his voice.

Dotty drew a deep breath and prompted, "And that made you snap. You wanted to hurt her. To prove you were just as much of a man as Gifford. That you could swing a bat…"

"Yes. Yes, that's right."

Ned jumped to his feet.

"I swung the bat like this. As hard as I could." He mimicked the motion as he spoke. "And I…"

Ned froze, his arms raised. His eyes glazing over.

Dotty could tell he was no longer focused on her. Or anyone in the pavilion. He was back there, with Pip, watching her fall.

In a voice full of astonishment, he cried, "I killed her."

CHAPTER FORTY

KEYA

Keya stopped talking to Sujin, Lynn and Zach as she watched Ned jump to his feet.

He called out, swinging his arms as if holding an imaginary cricket bat.

"As hard as I could," he exclaimed.

Lynn, Sujin and Zach all turned to stare at him.

Despite the continuing celebrations after the county cricket match, a hush fell over the members' pavilion as everyone's attention focused on Ned.

"I killed her!" he shouted.

Keya felt a strange mix of relief and sorrow. Ned sounded shocked, amazed even by what he'd done. Dotty had been right about many things, not least that Pip's death hadn't been premeditated. Ned had clearly acted in the heat of the moment.

And now he would carry the weight of that choice for the rest of his life.

Ned crumpled to the floor.

"Give him space," Aunt Beanie called, although no one had moved.

Sujin and Lynn stepped forward.

Dotty made to rise, but then sat back down heavily. Zach rushed across to her.

Keya was surprised when Georgina stood and moved to her side.

"I feel sorry for Ned," she said. "I used to think death, especially when one person inflicts it on another, was a black and white affair. But it's not always that clear, or easy to define."

"You've learned that from your experience abroad?" Keya enquired. She'd heard Georgina had solved a case while valuing a collection of antiques on an island in the Atlantic.

"Yes. On São Miguel, in the Azores. It was a close-knit community, and any trouble rippled through it causing more problems. That's why it had to be resolved quickly. But here? If only Ned had waited. If Pip had been given the chance to explain herself, outside the pressure of the cricket festival... maybe they could have sorted things out." She gave a slow shake of her long blonde hair.

"If you keep solving mysteries, you'll find the motives are often the same," Keya responded. "Love, greed, and revenge. But the reasons... those vary wildly. And when secrets and lies are involved, things get muddled. Misunderstood."

Keya watched as Zach helped Dotty to her feet. With a faint, sorrowful smile, Dotty turned to face her and Georgina.

"I stumbled across the culprit in my case," Georgina said, watching Dotty. "But Dotty? She drew that confession from Ned."

"Yes," Keya nodded. "After she helped Lynn interview the other potential suspects, she realised Ned was the most likely one."

"Especially after that punch he gave Adrian," Georgina agreed.

Zach and Dotty joined them, and Zach slid a protective arm around Dotty's waist.

"That's done then," he said quietly.

"Yes, and you were brilliant." Keya smiled encouragingly at Dotty.

"I don't feel any better for it," Dotty replied, her voice subdued. "But I suppose justice has to be done. For Pip. That's what matters. Still... it all seems rather unnecessary. If only Ned had waited. If only they'd had a proper conversation..."

Her voice trailed off.

"That's exactly what Georgina said," Keya murmured.

Just then, Warren and Thomas entered the pavilion.

Warren made straight for Lynn, who was watching as Sujin helped Ned onto a chair.

Thomas joined Keya and her group.

He looked straight at his Aunt Georgina. "We've been interviewing witnesses all afternoon. And you'll never guess what one of them said."

Keya had a feeling Georgina might, but she humoured her nephew as she said, "Go on, tell me."

Eyes wide with triumph, Thomas revealed, "He saw Ned hit Pip with the old cricket bat Gifford bought at the auction."

CHAPTER FORTY-ONE

DOTTY

Dotty drove past the popular Cotswold Wildlife Park where she knew families would be enjoying themselves on another wonderfully sunny July afternoon.

She'd driven this route many times but today felt different.

The countryside looked as glorious as ever. Wildflowers dotted the verge. A deep purple knapweed with its spiky, thistle-like flowers sat amongst a patch of tall oxeye daisies, their golden yellow centres turned to face the sun, and a scattering of yellow bird's-foot trefoil hugged the shorter grass beside the road.

It was no good pretending this was just another afternoon drive.

She had put off this conversation with Zach about whether he was going to continue renting his lovely house in Burford for as long as she could, using the cricket tournament as an excuse. He'd been patient, and even the rental agency had given him a few extra weeks' grace. But now a decision had to be made.

She knew what Zach wanted. He'd told her, plainly and without pressure, that he wanted more from this, and from them. A future together. A commitment.

And what had she done? Waffled. Dodged. Mumbled something about needing time.

Not because she didn't care. If anything, she cared too much. And that was the problem.

Zach wasn't like Al. He never tried to control her or make her feel small. He listened. He waited. He supported her. But still, she'd battled with herself, and with the outside world, for the freedom and independence she'd now gained, and she was loath, even scared, to give up. Could freedom and commitment truly live side by side? Could she let someone in without losing the parts of herself she had fought so hard to reclaim?

She glanced down at the spotty tin on the passenger seat which held a freshly baked Victoria sponge, topped with slices of fresh strawberries. She had made it for him.

Because it was time.

She had to face Zach.

Not out of fear of losing him, but because being with him felt… right. Unexpected, yes. Uneasy at times. But quietly, and importantly, right.

She slowed for the roundabout with the busier A40 before continuing straight on into Burford. Then she turned left into a quieter lane that led to Zach's honey-coloured stone house. The type of home she'd once dreamt about living in, with a colourful front garden, a practical rear vegetable patch, and, to one side, a long-established orchard with apple, plum, and cherry trees.

His solid black Jeep was parked on the gravel drive and Dotty pulled in beside it. She took a deep breath before lifting the cake tin and climbing out of her car.

Zach greeted her at the back door, or at least he waited, smiling softly as she walked towards him. He kissed her gently on the cheek.

"Thank you for coming," he murmured.

"I brought a cake," she replied, rather lamely.

"Wonderful. Why don't you sit in the garden, and I'll bring it out with the tea. Is Darjeeling all right with you?"

Dotty nodded as Zach took the cake tin from her. She was grateful as her hands were trembling.

Noticing, Zach clasped his free hand gently around one of them and gave it a reassuring squeeze.

On the freshly mown lawn, Zach had set up a small white wrought iron table with four matching chairs. There was already a jug of water with lemon slices and a sprig of elderflower floating in it, and a plate of scones with a jar of raspberry jam and a pot of clotted cream beside it.

Her tummy clenched. Not in fear, but in gratitude.

Instead of sitting, and to quell the rapid beating of her heart and the anxious thoughts racing through her head, she wandered along the flower border. She knew Zach employed a gardener to keep things in check, but it looked wonderful. Tidy, but wild enough to resemble a proper English cottage garden.

And what a joy to see bees buzzing around the fragrant stems of lavender, with the soft scent of pink-petalled roses lingering behind them.

"Here's the tea. I'll just go back for your cake. It looks fabulous, by the way." Zach set down a white teapot and milk jug and left again.

He was certainly making it difficult for her to refuse him. Al would never have considered what flavour of tea she might prefer, never mind buy scones and fresh cream. But Zach had considered every detail.

"Here we go. I thought it would be easier to cut us both a slice rather than bring out the whole cake, but if you want more…" he said, as he returned and sat down.

"No, that's wonderful. And I really should leave space for a scone."

Zach beamed. "I thought you'd like them. They're fresh from a local bakery."

He gestured for Dotty to sit.

Taking a deep breath, she did.

As Zach poured the tea into two mugs with birds on them, he said gently, "I'm sorry to put you on the spot like this, but we agreed a while ago to be honest with each other. I have given you time and…"

His words trailed off as Dotty placed her hand over his. Slowly, she shook her head. Then the words tumbled out.

"It's not you who should apologise. You've been patient and kind, and you've done everything I've asked of you. Agreeing to stay in the UK after finishing the mystery of your grandfather was a huge sacrifice. Moving down to be close to me in the Cotswolds was another. And then there's Akemans, in which you've invested both time and money. I can't ask you to do more when all you need from me is the truth, and to know that I not only appreciate all that you've done, but that I'm grateful."

As she paused for breath, Zach extracted his hand from under hers and passed her a teacup. "There's nothing you need to be grateful for," he said quietly.

"Oh, there is," Dotty protested. "So much. My life… I could never have imagined it would be like this. That I could be like this. Managing an important business, helping solve police cases, spending time with a group of wonderful friends. And…"

She looked up at Zach. Her heart lifted — expanded — as she finished, "…and falling in love with a patient, kind, and extremely handsome man."

Zach didn't speak straight away. He curled his fingers gently around hers, and for a moment, he just looked at her.

Then a smile spread slowly across his face. It started in his eyes, and gradually his whole face lit up.

"You've no idea how long I've waited to hear that," he said softly. "And I wasn't sure I ever would."

Dotty gave a shy smile, her nerves still sending sparks of adrenaline through her body.

"I was worried I'd left it too late."

"No, your timing is perfect," Zach said, his voice full of a quiet certainty that made her chest tighten. "I don't need fireworks, Dotty. Just this. You and me. Tea in this beautiful garden, and maybe a few slices of that cake."

Dotty laughed, catching herself off guard. Then, without quite meaning to, she placed her free hand over his and squeezed. "Then I suppose I'd better start getting used to this lovely house."

"You mean it?"

"I do," she said. "But we take things slowly."

Zach smiled reassuringly. "One step at a time," he said. "No lies. No hiding. Just the truth between us."

CHAPTER FORTY-TWO

KEYA

Keya was proud to be hosting the Coln Akeman Larks' celebratory dinner at her Waterwheel Cafe. The evening was in honour of Pip Lawton, without whom they wouldn't have secured their victory.

"It looks grand," said Barry, the landlord of The Axeman, as he wheeled in two boxes of wine on a hand trolley.

"Is this the first time you've been here?" asked Zivah, folding napkins into neat triangles.

"Yes. Never had a reason to visit before," he replied matter-of-factly, and then added, "That's all the booze. Two cases of wine, and a mix of beers and lagers from the Cotswold Lakes Brew Company."

"And we'll serve homemade lemonade and elderflower spritzers," Zivah confirmed with a smile.

"How many are we expecting?" Barry asked, glancing around at the three circular tables dressed in white linen, with an array of sparkling glassware and polished cutlery set out on them. Each one held a vase of summer garden flowers which Dotty had provided.

"All the players, plus their partners and families. And Dotty and Zach," Keya replied. "And since we're dedicating the dinner to Pip, we also invited a few people who knew her from her earlier cricketing days. Adrian didn't bother to reply, but Gifford, Harriet, Clare and

Cliff are all coming. Clare and Gifford even sent touching notes when they accepted. I think Pip would be glad we're gathering to remember her."

"It's just a shame Ned can't be here," declared Aunt Beanie as she swept into the cafe in a long velvet indigo jacket, complimented by a deep magenta scarf tied stylishly around her head.

"That would hardly be appropriate," Clara muttered. She and Marion had followed Aunt Beanie and Norman into the cafe.

"No," Beanie conceded. "But the whole thing is just so wretched."

To shift the mood, Keya added, "Lynn's coming tonight. And Warren."

"That was thoughtful to invite them," Marion said. "What can we do to help?"

Everyone clapped as Gifford finished his warm, amusing speech.

Keya leaned toward Sujin and whispered, "Wasn't that lovely? Hearing more about Pip and her short but remarkable career?"

"And she brought that same spirit to us," he replied, "helping us win the Three Counties Ladies' Cricket Cup."

Gifford raised his glass.

"To Philippa, or Pip, as you all affectionately knew her. Hip hip ..."

"Hooray!" the guests called out in unison.

The meal had been a triumph. Smoked trout pâté on slices of sourdough bread from a local bakery, followed by lemon and herb roast chicken with summer vegetables in a mustard crème fraîche sauce. And Mick had outdone himself in the kitchen with beautiful individual meringue nests, filled with whipped cream and summer fruits for pudding.

As Gifford sat down to another round of applause, Harriet rose slowly to her feet and lifted her hand for quiet.

"I'm pleased to announce," she began, "that the Three Counties Ladies' Cup will now be renamed in honour of Pip, to become the Philippa Lawson Cup. And I hope you, as the current holders, will return to defend it next year."

The applause was respectful but more subdued as Harriet sat down.

Keya thought Aunt Beanie spoke for them all when she declared, "Truth be told, I think we should retire with the win to our name, the cup on our shelf, and Pip properly honoured."

A Pantomime of Peril

It's pantomime season in the Cotswolds… but this year's performance is a real killer!

Winter has settled over the Cotswolds, and Dotty Sayers and her friends are in the spotlight as part of the local amateur dramatics pantomime production of *Jack and the Beanstalk.* With costumes to sew, lines to memorise, and rehearsals to juggle, the village is buzzing with excitement.

But on opening night, the show comes to an abrupt halt when a cast member dies on stage. As whispers of foul play sweep through the audience, Dotty and her friend Keya are drawn into a mystery that's anything but make-believe.

With suspects lurking in the wings and a tangle of alibis to unravel, the pair must tread carefully to uncover the truth. Can they solve the case before the final curtain falls, or will the killer steal the show?

Take your seat for a charming performance of *A Pantomime of Peril* today!

Scan the QR Code to Claim Your Copy of A Pantomime of Peril

Hour is Come

Would you like to know how Dotty and Keya first met? And read about Dotty's very first case, and discover what led her to solving murders and learning about antiques?

You can find out in *Hour is Come,* which is yours to keep when you sign up for my newsletter.

Scan the QR Code to Read Hour is Come for FREE

Inheritance and Intrigue in the Cotswolds

Grappling with self-doubt after the death of her husband, Marcus, Georgina Carey begins to rebuild her life—one mystery at a time.

In this **FREE prequel**, Georgina discovers a sapphire ring in

Marcus' safe. Determined to return it, she soon finds herself caught between two women—both claiming it as their own.

As tensions rise and betrayals come to light, she unearths secrets tied to an unsolved death.

Can she expose the truth before the past tears a family apart?

Scan the QR Code to Read Inheritance and Intrigue in the Cotswolds for FREE

If you enjoyed this book, please tell someone you know. And for those people you don't know, leave a review to help them decide whether or not to read it.

Leave a review on Amazon

For more information visit VictoriaTait.com

UNTITLED

Printed in Dunstable, United Kingdom

65472567R00117